The Gypsy Quest

The Gypsy Quest

Copyright © William Carr 2018 All Rights Reserved

Spiderwize
Remus House
Coltsfoot Drive
Woodston
Peterborough
PE2 9BF

www.spiderwize.com

A CIP catalogue record for this book is available from the British Library.

ISBN: 978-1-911596-85-1

THE GYPSY QUEST

WILLIAM CARR

SPIDERWIZE
Peterborough UK
2018

Elements of the Manuscript

The protagonists in the story are Chris and Mirela who find themselves being pursued relentlessly by a group of villains who are determined to capture Chris and extract from him certain information that he unknowingly possesses.

Mirela befriends Chris, and with her extraordinary gift of insight she is able to help him evade capture. Chris and Mirela are given protection by Rosanna, Mirela's maternal grandmother, and her uncle, Joseph, who is a former MI5 agent. There is an attempt to kidnap Chris from the school that he attends with Mirela, and they flee to a cave where they are able to hide, but later, when they are discovered there, they almost become entombed in the cave when they try to escape the clutches of the villains.

They try to hide with a travelling Gypsy band, but again they are discovered. They endeavour to escape to France in a hot air balloon, but the balloon crashes. They take shelter with a fisherman in the village of Clovelly and from there they are taken to the Scilly Isles where they are able to board a schooner and set sail for Jersey. The schooner almost capsizes in a storm, but they survive and are able to land in Jersey. They take shelter in the Corbiere Lighthouse where Chris is almost taken by a group of men impersonating the crew of a rescue craft.

Finally, they are transported to an isolated house on the western side of the island. There, they are located once again by the villains and both children are taken through a tunnel connected to the property, to a wartime gun-site where the villains intend to extract the information Chris possesses. There is a mighty battle when the gun-site is stormed by security forces.

Unfortunately, there is the added complication of an entity which protects the gun-site from intruders that causes havoc with the villains and the security forces. Mirela and her grandmother unite their psychic power and battle with the entity before it is able to destroy everyone. The eventual outcome is that Chris finds out that he has unknowingly given the villains flawed information and the formula extracted from him is useless.

Chapter One

Mirela, as much as she tried, couldn't pay attention to what the teacher was saying. Normally she was very attentive in class, but today she was watching the new boy very closely. He looked quite pale and appeared very quiet; but then, everyone was quiet on their first day at a new school. He was to the front of the class and two rows away from where Mirela sat. What had caught her attention was his aura, the light that radiates about the head and shoulders of people; his was flickering weakly in a most unusual way. She felt a tingle of concern. When this happened, she knew it was a sign that the person was ill, or deeply troubled. She sensed that the teacher was looking her way, so she quickly returned her attention to the lesson in hand, making a mental note to approach the new boy in some way to try to get him to talk so she could find out more about him.

Her opportunity came at lunch time. Mirela waited until the new boy had joined the queue in the dining hall then she stood behind him. When she had been served she approached him as he stood with his tray, hesitating, undecided as to where he should go.

"You can sit anywhere you like, you know," said Mirela. "But if you want to come with me I will show you a place to sit."

She took him to an empty table where they set down their

trays and were soon tucking hungrily into the food that had been served to them.

"First day is always the worst at a new school, especially if you don't know anyone," said Mirela, sympathetically. "Where are you from?"

The boy looked up from his plate and stared silently at Mirela. She returned his stare, but more because she found his appearance so unusual, with his deep blue eyes and his flaxen hair, he looked more like an angel from one of the many picture books she had read.

"I used to live in London, but I'm staying with my aunt and uncle now until my parents return," he said, quietly.

"That's interesting," said Mirela with a smile. "I'm living with my grandparents waiting for my parents to come back too. My name is Mirela. What's yours?" she asked.

"Chris."

"Pleased to meet you Chris," said Mirela, holding out her hand.

Chris laid down his knife and placed his hand in Mirela's, but when he tried to take his hand back she held on to it, firmly. Mirela felt small burning sensations emanating from certain parts of Chris's palm. She had expected this and knew that visible marks of these sensations, which she could read, would appear on her palm for several days. Chris refrained from snatching his hand back. This girl, Mirela, was really the only person who had spoken to him and offered the promise of friendship. If she wanted to hold his hand, then that was OK. He liked what he saw, but she puzzled him. She was as tall as him and slim. Her pretty face was framed by long dark hair, and her complexion had a slight olive tone to it. The most unusual thing about her were her eyes. They were an intense green colour, and although she was looking his way, they appeared not to be focused on him.

"Sorry – I didn't mean to hold on for so long," said Mirela, releasing his hand.

"That's all right," said Chris, giving her a curious look. "Now that we have introduced ourselves, I hope we can become friends."

"Yes – I would like that," she replied, solemnly.

***

Chris was unused to attending a co-ed school. His previous school had been an all boys' establishment, and he didn't quite know what to make of the girls he had come into contact with. He missed the boisterous, rough and tumble relationship of his chums, and the emphasis on sport that had been so much a part of the school curriculum. Then suddenly he had had to leave St Martin's for safety's sake.

The closed atmosphere of the Government Laboratories where his parents worked had been a dismal place. There had been very few activities for the children to become involved in, other than the lessons taught by tutors who were bussed in daily. In contrast, this new school seemed to have the potential to please. He had brightened visibly when he had heard that the next period was to be football.

Mirela paused in her work to glance over at Chris. His aura seemed a lot brighter and he seemed to be quite absorbed with the work they had been given concerning English monarchs.

Mirela remembered all too well the way she had fretted when she had first started school. Her grandmother had comforted her when she had pined for her Gypsy life on the road and had explained to her that an education was an essential thing to have in this day and age. The world was changing, and if the Romany people wanted their way of life to continue, then they must encourage their young people to become learned and to know the laws of the land. Mirela eventually adjusted to school life, but in her own way.

One day, shortly after she had started school, Mirela had been told that the next day was a Mufti Day and that the pupils didn't have to wear their uniform. Not really understanding what 'mufti' meant, she had arrived in class dressed in her traditional Gypsy garb, which had caused a minor sensation amongst the pupils and teachers alike. When the head explained what mufti was, Mirela had thought about it for a moment, then suggested:

"Why not make it a fun day and allow the pupils to choose a mode of dress, traditional or otherwise, and have a competition with a small prize for the winner?"

The head, taken aback, had discussed it with his staff and they had judged it to be a rather refreshing change. And so, it came about. Things were never quite the same after Mirela started attending the Silian Village School.

Mirela waited patiently for Chris to appear. She had seen him trooping with the rest of the boys from the sports field where they had played football for their last period. She had asked him to come to tea at the farm and to meet her grandparents. It would also give her another opportunity to perhaps find out what was troubling him.

Once again, she examined the red marks on her palm that had been made when she had held Chris's hand. She was intrigued by the square sign that appeared on the line that ruled the head, on the thumb side of the palm, a square sign was a symbol of protection. The triangle on the edge of the palm, below the little finger, was also a complimentary positive sign. But the spot shape, low on the palm, opposite the thumb, was another thing. Mirela knew she must probe very gently for information or she might frighten him off before he fully understood that she only wanted to help him.

For some hours now, she had had a nagging feeling that something was about to happen, something threatening. It had grown stronger as the day wore on and she knew that she mustn't ignore it any longer. With her senses highly tuned, she had been noticing things that ordinarily would have gone unnoticed. There was the car that had been driven slowly past the school several times while the children were in the playground. There was the shadowy figure, amongst the trees opposite the school that seemed to be peering through a pair of binoculars, watching everything. Somehow, she knew that this stealthy activity must have something to do with Chris. It was time to warn him.

Seeing Mr Jones, the caretaker, leading the last of the pupils towards the main gate, Mirela ran and caught up with Chris who was last in line.

"Hi! Mirela," he grinned, his eyes bright and his face red from his football exertions. "What's for tea?"

She remained silent, and as they passed through the gate she glanced apprehensively towards the opposite side of the road. She gasped and stopped suddenly, causing Chris to bump into her. A man had appeared and was running towards them from out of the trees.

Chapter Two

Mirela, turning swiftly, grabbed hold of Chris and started dragging him back to the gate, but the man was fast, and he was soon upon them. He shoved Mirela out of the way and taking hold of Chris lifted him, intending to sling him over his shoulder, but Chris, yelling and struggling violently, caused the man to stop to get a firmer grip on him. Taken aback by the suddenness of it all, Mr Jones was slow to react. Then, recovering from his surprise, he charged out of the school gate furious that anyone should attack any one of the school children. He launched himself at the man, hooked an arm around his neck and pulled him backward. Staggering off balance the man released his hold on Chris who fell sprawling on the ground, but he was up in a flash and dashing with Mirela back into the school grounds. At the same moment a large, black car sped to a stop, tyres squealing, a short distance from the gate. Two men jumped out and as they approached the man struggling with Mr Jones he shouted, "The boy – get the boy."

Mirela, watching the brave caretaker being thrown to the ground by the much bigger man, knew she couldn't help Mr Jones. She must prevent the men getting through the gate. She snatched the padlock with the keys in it and slid the bolt home. Quickly, she fixed the padlock into the bolt and locked it in place with the key. With the gate secured she turned to flee as one of the men crashed into it and stretched a hand through the bars to grab her. Fingers raked through her hair, grasping a few strands, jerking her head back, but she managed to pull free, leaving some of her tresses behind in the man's fist. For a fleeting moment Mirela glanced back towards where Mr Jones was staggering to his feet. He looked shaken, but otherwise seemed unhurt.

"I'm sorry Mr Jones," she called.

The caretaker lifted his head and looked in her direction, he raised a hand and gestured for her to go. She raced to where Chris was waiting, his eyes wide with fright, and grasped his hand. They ran as fast as they could around the side of the school building and out of the rear gate into the open countryside, taking the path that led across the fields toward her grandparent's farm.

***

Mirela was born into the Lovell Romany Gypsy tribe. The only child of Seth and Carmen Lovell, who, uncommon for Gypsies, had attended university and had later established thriving careers for themselves in London. By the time she was five they recognized that their daughter had inherited the gift. It was decided that London was not the ideal place to be brought up, so she was taken to live with her delighted grandparents on their farm in Wales.

Fleeing persecution in Spain, the Lovells had come to Britain in the seventeenth century and had established a travelling circuit between England and Wales. The men had earned their livelihood in knife grinding, rearing horses and farm work, whilst the women went from door to door, selling pegs and telling fortunes. The disruption of the Second World War didn't have much of an effect upon their way of life and except for the occasional dogfight in the skies above, or the sound of artillery defences during bombing raids, things were much the same as they had always been. Perhaps the only difference was the racially motivated criticism suggesting that Gypsies were not contributing to the war effort, but few knew that some of the young men had joined the armed forces and of course, Gypsies worked the land helping to produce the food the nation so desperately needed.

Ever since Mirela could remember, she had been able to see auras. They appeared in as many colours and shades as there are in a rainbow, differing from person to person. Some people had red auras, some blue, others green. There were also those who had yellow, orange, violet or pink auras depending on what kind of person they were. Some auras were clear while others were fuzzy, subject to whether the person was happy or worried or contented. Sickness, dejection, love, fulfilment, these all reflected on how strong or how weak an aura could be. Mirela had accepted this as normal, thinking everyone could see what she saw, not knowing that very few people possessed this gift.

Her growing ability to sense danger would also prove to be advantageous should Chris suffer another attempted kidnapping.

Chapter Three

The children raced across the fields, through barred gates and over stiles, not stopping for anything. Approaching a small wood, they heard a crashing in the undergrowth and froze, afraid that they had blundered into a trap. They turned to flee, but the next moment a large deer broke cover. It stopped and looked at them in surprise but was soon lost from view as it sped away into the trees. Chris gave a nervous laugh.

"Whew! I really thought we..."

Mirela held up her hand for silence. She cocked her head sideways, listening intently, her eyes again unfocussed as though looking inward. Suddenly, she snapped her head up and stared in the direction of a distant hill. Chris, unsure of what was going on, glanced nervously in the same direction, his eyes widening when he saw two horsemen unexpectedly appear on the skyline. The men halted their horses while one swept the area with a pair of binoculars. Fixing his gaze on one spot he said something to his companion and pointed in the direction of the children. Immediately, they spurred their horses and began to move off down the hill at a fast gallop.

"Come on Chris, follow me, I know a place where we can hide," Mirela called urgently, as she sprinted down into a small hollow and following a fast-flowing river, raced along its bank toward the distant sound of rushing water.

They could hear the tattoo of hooves as the horsemen drew closer, adding further urgency to their need for haste. Where the path became choked and overgrown they found they had to climb up towards the trail which the horsemen would use, wasting precious minutes in their attempt to put as much distance between themselves and their pursuers as possible. Mirela glanced over her shoulder to see Chris was struggling to keep up.

They were both breathing hard and were slowing as the pace began to tell on them.

The drumming of the hooves on the trail above was frighteningly close now. They heard a shout and then a crashing amongst the trees up ahead as one of the horsemen plunged with his steed down into the hollow to head them off, then the sound of the other horseman closing in behind them. The children stopped, knowing they were trapped. Chris sunk to his knees panting for breath, a look of exhaustion on his face. Mirela, not willing to give up, looked frantically around for a way out. The only immediate means of escape was the river, but she was not a strong swimmer, and not knowing if Chris could swim, it presented a desperate choice.

The decision was taken out of her hands as the horseman who was heading them off suddenly appeared, looming high above them. Unable to control his steed's descent, he hurled towards Mirela, who, frozen to the spot, instinctively closed her eyes and clasped her hands preparing for the impact. At the last moment the horseman, cursing his steed loudly, hauled on the reins and managed to swing his horse away from Mirela, but in doing so the horse's rump struck her a glancing blow, throwing her into the fast-flowing river.

Chris, a good swimmer, didn't hesitate. He dived into the river and struck out for Mirela who was struggling to keep her head above the surface. Reaching her he held on to her as they were carried around a bend. But soon, another danger threatened as Chris realized they were being swept towards a waterfall. He looked around searching for an outcrop, something that they could grab a hold of to prevent themselves being swept over the brink. But there was nothing. All they could hope for was that there was deep water below the falls and no rocks that could injure them.

Suddenly, the world dropped away as they plunged over the edge of the falls and for a brief moment they were suspended in space. They dropped into a deep pool and struggled to the surface moments later, spluttering and gasping for air. Chris reached out for Mirela and started to pull her to the bank, but she shook her head, shrugging off his assistance and struggled to the opposite side where she pulled herself onto a flat rock and lay panting for breath, completely spent. Puzzled, he followed her and waited for her to recover her strength. Her face was pallid, and a trickle of blood came from a swollen nose. Moving to her side he took her hand, an anxious look on his face, but before he could say anything the dreaded beat of horse's hooves, approaching swiftly, hastened them into taking to their heels again. Mirela struggled to her feet holding her arm and wincing as she did so and beckoned Chris to follow her. She led him clambering along a ledge that ran under the falls. She seemed to suddenly disappear in front of his eyes, but when he reached the spot where she had vanished he found a hidden fold in the rock face and behind that was a narrow fissure. He passed through the opening into quite a large cavern and joined Mirela in the semi-darkness as she slumped against a wall and slid to the floor. He went to her and laid a hand on her shoulder.

"Are you all right Mirela?" he asked, looking at her with concern. "That was quite a thump you took from the horse. Are you hurt?"

"No – I'm all right, just feeling a bit faint. It's a good thing it was the horse's rump and not its hooves that struck me, or it could have been much worse."

They hugged each other, both trembling with the cold and their reaction to their escape from the horsemen.

Mirela handed Chris a blanket. "You had best get out of those wet things before you catch a chill," she said. "Wring them out and hang them up to dry. We are quite safe here. The men will be looking for us in the river and when they don't find us they may think we have drowned."

Chris took the blanket and moved self-consciously deeper into the recesses of the cave to strip off. Mirela lit a candle and they huddled close to each other, listening to the muted sound of cascading water. They stared up at the shadowy shapes thrown onto the cavern walls by the guttering light of the candle. Monsters, animals and angels could be imagined as they took shape, only to disappear when the slightest breath of air caused the flame to waver mysteriously.

"How do you know this place?" asked Chris, curiously.

"This is my secret place where I come when I want to be alone," explained Mirela. "You're the only other person who knows about it now, other than my dad and my grandmother. Dad discovered it when he was a boy and used to come here to fish and kept his fishing tackle in here until he became too big to squeeze through the opening. Then he showed it to me."

Chris looked around him taking in the crude sticks of furniture that had probably been cobbled together by Mirela's father. A long bench, on which they sat, a small table that held the candle, and a stool completed the chattels that filled the interior of the cavern. Occasionally, the scuttling of small creatures could be heard as they moved about in the darker recesses of the cavern. Mirela, who had closed her eyes briefly, sensed that Chris was studying her surreptitiously.

"What?" she exclaimed.

"How do you do that? How did you know that the man outside

the school was after me? And how did you know that the horsemen were chasing us before they appeared?"

Mirela was silent for a moment. If she told Chris about herself, perhaps he would in turn tell her why he was so troubled and explain why he was being pursued so relentlessly. She took a deep breath, "I come from a long line of Romany Gypsies..."

***

Chris stared at Mirela in wonder. "I would find all that you have told me hard to believe if I hadn't seen it with my own eyes. Can you really see auras?"

"Yes."

"Can you see mine?"

"Yes."

"What colour is it?"

"It's a bright, pale blue, fading to orange at the edges."

"Is that a good thing?"

"It's an improvement on what it was like when I first saw you. Your aura was quite weak then. It's what attracted me to you in the first place. I could tell you were deeply troubled."

"You could tell that by just looking at my aura?"

"Yes – now give me your hand – your right one."

Chris placed his hand in Mirela's. She studied his palm for a few moments then began tracing the lines, the mounts and the markings with her finger while murmuring in a strange language. After several minutes she closed his hand and looked up, a thoughtful expression on her face.

"Well – do I get to have my fortune told?" he asked, with a smile.

"It's not really that simple," she said, making an excuse. "I really need to study up on my palmistry before I can give you an answer. Now, when are you going to tell me what these people want with you?"

Chris hesitated. He had sworn not to tell anyone why he was living in Wales and why he was not with his parents. But Mirela had taken such risks to help keep him out of the clutches of those who wanted to capture him that he felt she had a right to know.

"What I am about to tell you, Mirela, must go no further. Will you swear to keep it a secret and tell no one?"

"I swear," she vowed solemnly.

"My father is a scientist who came to England from Sweden," Chris began. "He met my mother when they both worked for the same government department. The work was top secret and when there was a breakthrough in the research that was being carried out, my father was instrumental in discovering the formula for a new form of energy that would revolutionise the aerodynamics industry."

He went on to tell her how some news had leaked out about the discovery. Agents, from an as yet unknown source, had begun to target his father and there had been several attempts to infiltrate the government departments security. Their home had been ransacked and most of their possessions smashed in the process, and a foiled attempt to kidnap his parents had resulted in them having to go into hiding. Chris had been sent to stay with his aunt and uncle where it was thought it would be safe for him to continue with his education. But now it looked like they were trying to kidnap him, so they could put pressure on his father to give up the formula.

Mirela stayed silent as she absorbed what Chris had revealed to her. She soon came to the conclusion that there was no alternative but for Chris to also go into hiding too.

Darkness had fallen when the children stepped cautiously out of the cave and made their way carefully along the ledge to the bank. The full moon had turned the scene into a magical wonderland of shimmering, rushing water, spilling long translucent shards of light into a luminous pool of broken crystal. The surrounding trees cast ominous, deep pools of broken shadow upon the river bank that had the children casting apprehensive glances about them as they quickly made their way along the path, ears pricked for any threatening sound, fearful that they would be pounced upon at any moment. Soon, they could see the lights of the farm in the distance and their pace quickened noticeably as they pushed on towards the shelter and safety that they so desperately needed.

Chapter Four

There was silence at the table when Mirela and Chris finished describing the harrowing details of their escape from the kidnappers. There was an air of deep concern that carried with it a furious anger against those who had attempted to take the two children. Chris's uncle, who had arrived at the farm with his aunt when summoned by Mirela's grandmother, was first to speak.

"My brother hinted that there was some sort of trouble concerning the work he was doing when he brought young Chris to stay with us, but I certainly didn't think it would be anything like this. We must inform the police, who will be still searching for the children, that they are safe, and we must quickly make plans to deal with this situation."

Mirela's grandmother, noting how pale Mirela looked, made a decision. "All that will have to wait until after I have taken my granddaughter to the hospital. She may have sustained other injuries from her collision with the horse, besides the one to her collarbone. Come child, I will ask Sam to drive us there."

Sam, the resident farm hand, lived in the annexe next to the farmhouse. He had lived and worked on the farm since leaving school some five years previously and was looked upon as one of the family, which thereby entitled him to use Mirela's grandmother's first name, Rosanna. He had a passion for automobiles and could often be found servicing the farm tractor in his spare time or tinkering under the bonnet of his car preparing it for one of the many rallies he often attended.

Arriving at the hospital, Sam was instructed by Rosanna to visit the police station to inform them that the children had found their way back to the farm and were safe. After a thorough examination a nurse dressed Mirela's left arm in a supporting sling, then she was declared fit enough to return home, but instructed to have plenty of rest which would allow the soreness of the bruising to fade and give the break in her collarbone time to mend. Sam was waiting for them when they left the hospital and gunned the powerful engine as they climbed into the car.

"Back to the farm Sam, but not too fast, Mirela is nursing a broken collarbone," cautioned Rosanna. "So, try to avoid any potholes along the way."

Sam acknowledged the caution and kept the speed at a steady thirty miles per hour. Almost half way back to the farm their headlights picked out a car in the darkness that was blocking the road ahead, and a policeman approaching waving a torch and signalling for them to stop. Coming to a halt, Sam wound down his window and asked the policeman what the problem was.

"Just routine, sir," answered the policeman, shining his torch in Sam's face, then into the rear of the car where Rosanna and Mirela sat. The policeman signalled to his colleagues and several of them approached to join him. "Can you identify yourself and tell me where you are from?"

Before Sam could answer he felt Rosanna grip his arm and hiss a warning. "Get us out of here Sam. These are not the police."

It took several seconds for Sam to react then he flung the car into reverse and slammed the accelerator pedal to the floor. The tyres screeched, spinning madly, then gripped and the car hurtled backward gathering speed with every yard. Sam, twisting in his seat to look out of the rear window, gripped the steering wheel with one hand and held the handbrake with the other as the car rocketed back along the lane until they came to a track that led off into a wood.

The car's rear end swung around as he spun the steering wheel and applied the handbrake, effectively bringing the car's nose to point towards the track, then stamping down on the accelerator they left the lane and flew deep into the wood. The car bumped and slithered as they careered at breakneck speed, following the track as it turned and twisted through the trees. Mirela whimpered with pain as the car jolted and shifted violently throwing her and her grandmother about in the back seat. Rosanna held on to Mirela and tried to cushion her from the worst of the jolts, but with little success. Sam, glancing in his driving mirror, knew when the pursuing car had entered the wood by the erratic behaviour of its headlights as it bounced along the track behind them. He had grown up near to this area, so he had some knowledge of the wood and what to expect from the lay of the land.

A short distance ahead there was an escarpment that dropped away abruptly for about fifteen feet. There was a path that led to a narrow crevice that would allow a person to descend to the lower level, but the main track turned sharply to the right and followed the edge of the escarpment for about half a mile. Sam explained his plan to Rosanna and fifty metres before the escarpment he turned left on to a narrower track. Dowsing his lights, he travelled the last thirty metres in darkness and came to a halt behind a woodcutter's hut. Hidden from the main track they could see the lights and hear the approach of the pursuing car.

"Hold my hands Mirela and concentrate with me," whispered Rosanna. "We must obscure the way ahead to rid ourselves of these pursuers."

Mirela grasped her grandmother's hands and closing her eyes, breathed deeply and immediately felt her grandmother's powerful psychic force join with hers. Their linked psychic power gathered the tendrils of ground mist that wreathed like serpents amongst the trees and formed them into an impenetrable curtain that hid the dangerous drop from the escarpment. The pursuing car raced past the branch track where they were hidden and onward towards the escarpment. Moments later they heard the howl of the engine as the vehicle launched itself into space and then a loud crash as it hit the ground below the escarpment.

Sam started the engine and drove slowly from the wood to the lane that would take them back to the farm. Turning his head, he asked, curiously, "How did you know that those men were not the police?"

"They didn't reply in Welsh when you spoke to them," answered Rosanna, sharing a secret smile with Mirela who knew that it had been the darkness of the men's auras that had warned them of the men's questionable intentions.

When they had returned to the farm, Chris and his uncle and aunt greeted them with relief. The children, tired after their long and eventful day, were soon tucked up in bed. Mirela, still in pain and feeling drained after the effort of her psychic experience, fell into an exhausted sleep as soon as her grandmother had closed the door to her room. The adults, looking serious and thoughtful, gathered at the kitchen table to discuss the latest worrying developments.

"It looks like these people will stop at nothing to get to Chris," remarked Chris's uncle grimly. "Heaven knows what methods they would be prepared to use to obtain information of his whereabouts."

David Dudley, Rosanna's husband, a quiet unassuming man, spoke for the first time.

"Obviously, we must contact the police and ask for their protection. It's not safe here; they could be watching our every move. I won't be satisfied until we have found a safe place for the children, wherever that is."

Chris's uncle thumped the table with his fist. "Then so be

it. Tomorrow I will book a passage for the three of us to sail to America where we can stay with my sister until it is safe to return."

Rosanna, silent until now, disagreed with Chris's uncle. "I think we have been extremely lucky in avoiding the clutches of these people up to now. They seem to be well organized and very resourceful. I do agree that whoever they are, they will not stop until they get their hands on Chris. But I disagree with the idea of you taking Chris to another country. I think this will only delay them long enough for you to become complacent and think he is safe. What we want is a place where he can disappear completely."

Chris's uncle leaned forward, frowning belligerently. "Surely, you don't think that their influence would stretch to…"

Chris's aunt held up her hand and interrupted her husband.

"George, there is a lot we don't know. It would be wrong to assume that their influence would only be confined to Britain. I would like to hear more from Rosanna concerning the place where Chris could be safely hidden."

Rosanna hesitated, knowing that what she was about to say was going to be controversial. "There is a place where the children can be hidden. A place where they will be watched at all times. Mirela is to be included in these plans too, for she is almost in as much danger as Chris, owing to her helping him to escape capture. I cannot tell you where this place is. The less people who know, the safer it will be." Rosanna took a deep breath then resumed. "As much as I know that it will distress you, there must be no contact between you and Chris. What you don't know, you cannot divulge. Each of us is viewed as a source of information to these people. Therefore, we must each put in place a plan for our own personal security."

Chapter Five

After some discussion, Chris's aunt and uncle, knowing that they had little choice, reluctantly accepted the conditions of the plan that Rosanna had suggested. They decided that they would close their home in the village of Olwen and take a prolonged visit to America where it was hoped they would be much safer.

Meanwhile, Rosanna instructed Sam to take his car and search for a band of Gypsies who would be travelling the area between Newtown and Welshpool that was part of the circuit they followed each year. He was to give a message to the Chieftain that when they reached their traditional campsite near to the village of Silian in Cardiganshire, Rosanna, his friend, would contact him.

When Sam returned to the farm, he informed Rosanna that it would be some weeks before the Gypsy band arrived in the farm's vicinity. But yes, Ruben looked forward to seeing Rosanna again and would help her in any way that he could.

It took several days of complete rest before Mirela felt strong enough to leave the farmhouse. Then, she and Chris helped out in the general running of the farm by feeding the livestock, collecting eggs from the hen house and bringing the cattle in from the fields to be milked. Police cars parked at the gate and officers patrolling the pastures were visible evidence that the authorities were taking the threat of kidnapping seriously.

Plain-clothed policemen and men of military bearing came to question Rosanna and the children and left with signed statements that described the frightening encounters that had occurred between them and the shadowy men who were hunting them.

Obviously, the high level of security that was being provided could not go on indefinitely, and more lasting precautions would have to be put in place when the police were withdrawn. Rosanna decided that the cave under the falls was as good a temporary place as any to hide the children, so with their help she set about making the place a little more comfortable for them. They made numerous trips to the cave taking sleeping bags, food, books, lanterns and even a small stove upon which they could cook simple meals. The children could return to the farm during the hours of darkness, but if danger threatened, they would stay in the cave until it became safe to venture out again.

The long days of summer were spent exploring the banks of the river and watching the wildlife. To the delight of the children, a pair of kingfishers that had taken up residence close to the cave provided them with plenty of interest. Chris proved to have an eye for detail and was surprisingly good at sketching. While fishing he would spend hours studying the birds and would later draw them from memory. Mirela, still recuperating, read numerous books on many subjects, the contents of which she would often discuss with Chris. She found that he had an amazing memory and could recite poems and long passages from plays, often making her laugh with his antics while quoting something from the many works of Shakespeare that he had memorized. His profound and intellectual knowledge of many subjects impressed Mirela who was no slouch herself when it came to academic ability.

Rosanna would visit them daily, bringing fresh food and baked treats. She would sometimes stay with them and when shadows lengthened in the evening they would retire to the cave, which they had all contributed in trying to make as comfortable and as cosy as possible. As darkness gathered, a lamp would be lit, and the cave walls would once again exaggerate the size and movement of each shadow as they moved about doing their chores. It was then that the children would ask Rosanna for another tale about her life on the road when she had travelled the circuit with her Gypsy family.

Rosanna, a born story teller, would keep the children wide-eyed and enthralled with anecdotes about the characters and customs of the Gypsy clans. She told of the Locke Clan who had earned the name because they were good at picking the farmers' padlocked gates at night, so they could graze their horses. By morning they had moved on, and the farmers never knew. In the late nineteenth century, one of the Locke fought Seth Lovell over a disputed travelling circuit in north west Wales. Seth lost, so in accordance with Romany law he moved his family down to south Wales where the family still maintained their circuit.

One morning they rose early. Having decided to stay the night in the cave, they planned to visit one of their favourite spots on the riverbank to watch the early morning activities of a family of otters. Mirela had not slept well, she had been troubled by dreams and there was the persistent feeling that all was not well. Chris noticed her preoccupation and commented on it.

"Is there something bothering you, Mirela? You have that worried look about you again."

"You're beginning to know me too well," she answered, with a thin smile. "It's nothing I can put my finger on, but I think we should stay close to the cave today."

"Do you know what is going to happen and when it will happen?" asked Chris, with a look of concern on his face.

"No – premonitions don't work like that. It depends on how strong the feeling is as to how soon it will happen; it could be today, tomorrow, or next week, this one is becoming stronger by the hour."

Not wanting to be caught out in the open, they hurried back to the cave where they tried to occupy themselves, Mirela reading, while Chris fixed a new line to one of the fishing rods that he had found in the cave.

Mirela found it impossible to concentrate on her reading. The feeling of imminent danger was a constant nagging pulse in her mind. The most troubling part of the premonition was that there was an extra frightening element to it, a fierce, ravening, fury that made her quake and fear that their presence in such a confined area could prove to be perilous. Involuntarily, she slammed her book shut making the sound reverberate like a thunderclap around the walls of the cave. Chris, startled, dropped his rod and spun around. When he saw the alarm on Mirela's face he stepped towards her.

"What is it Mirela? What do you see?"

"Help me," she said urgently. "We must barricade the entrance – quickly."

They pulled the bench to the opening, struggled to stand it on end then pushed mightily to lodge it firmly into the fissure, effectively blocking the entrance to the cave. Chris jammed a log against the bench and wedged the other end against a raised spur in the uneven floor to reinforce the barrier. He grabbed one of the small stools with the intention of blocking a small gap in the barricade, but as he tried to place the stool in position a snarling, slavering head suddenly smashed into the gap and seized his arm in its jaws. Chris cried out in pain and fear as the dog tugged on his outstretched arm causing him to fall against the barrier.

The attack had come with such suddenness that Mirela was rooted to the spot with horror but hearing Chris's cries of pain and seeing his desperate struggle to beat the dog off, spurred her into action. The only thing on hand was a section of a fishing rod, the stout section with a cork hand grip. Sweeping it up she raced to Chris's side, but she hesitated, there was no room for her to swing at the dog's head. Instead, she knelt and looking along the rod she pushed it into a gap between Chris's arm and the dogs now bloodied fangs. Putting all of her weight behind the rod she lunged forward with all her strength. She felt the rod travel about six or eight inches down the dog's throat, lacerating it, the muffled snarls changed to squeals of pain as the animal, choking, let go of Chris's arm and withdrew its head.

Chris rolled away from the entrance clutching his torn arm, his face white with pain and shock. As reaction set in, he slumped to the floor in a dead faint while Mirela held a cloth against his arm to staunch the blood. Binding the wounds as best she could with strips torn from a pillowcase, she cradled his head in her lap and wiped his face gently with a damp cloth to help bring him around.

She could hear furtive movements on the other side of the barricade and the occasional whine of a dog, and then an order was given. The barricade creaked and moved a little but held as the men tried to force their way into the cave. The confined space made it difficult to manoeuvre and to get leverage against the barrier, and even if they managed to break through, none of the men would be small enough to pass through the fissure. But it would not stop the dogs.

"You in there," a voice called. "You know you're trapped. Take down the barricade. It's only a matter of time before we gain entrance, but if you make us wait we will send in the dogs."

Chris, recovering from his fainting spell, stood groggily leaning against the cave wall. He looked at his bandaged arm, winced, then looking up at Mirela he spoke despairingly.

"It looks like we're done for this time, Mirela. How do you think they knew where to find us?"

"They must have found something," Mirela reflected. "An article of clothing perhaps, with our scent on it, then used the tracker dogs. Can't begin to guess why they chose this area though. I thought we were safe here."

The man's voice called again, harsher this time.

"We only want you, Chris. If you come out now we will let the girl go."

Chris looked at Mirela resignedly. "We don't seem to have much choice."

"Don't even begin to think like that," said Mirela, ferociously. "They have no intention of letting me go. I know too much, and I would also be able to identify them after today."

A new voice, cajoling, and much closer to the entrance, summoned them.

"Come on children, you have nowhere to go. Remove the obstruction and I will see that you are well treated. All we want is for Chris to give us the information we seek, and you will be back with your families in no time."

Mirela looked questioningly at Chris, a slight frown furrowing her brow, but he turned away from her, unwilling to meet her gaze. She decided now was not the time to question him, perhaps later he would explain. Meanwhile, they had to do something, anything, to avoid capture.

Things went quiet for a few minutes, all that could be heard was the constant sound of the waterfall. Then there was a sudden renewed onslaught to remove the barrier. There was the thud of blades biting into wood and chips of wood flew about as the barricade was attacked with axes.

Chapter Six

Bruno Fletcher sat relaxing at a pavement café on the west bank in Paris. He glanced at his watch. He had purposely arrived early, so he could do some thinking and some planning before the people he was meeting arrived. Of medium height and stocky build, with crinkly dark hair above regular features and dressed smartly in a dark suit and tie, he could have passed for a typical businessman. However, a black patch over his left eye gave him a roguish look that belied the first impression. He had lost the eye when a lapse in concentration had allowed a female prisoner he was arresting, to slip off a stiletto-heeled shoe and use it as a weapon while attempting an escape. He had been cashiered out of Interpol several years later when it was found that he often brutalized the people he was arresting. When asked about his injury he would hint at some perilous conflict in the past and leave it to the questioner's imagination.

He looked around at the other tables, examining each person in turn. It was a habit he had instinctively acquired during his many years as a policeman, and later as an agent of Interpol. He always recognized if he was being shadowed. Something tangible about the person following him seemed to trigger his caution no matter how innocuous they seemed, and he was very seldom wrong. He glanced casually around him just like a tourist would do, then he suddenly stiffened. Across the road a figure had stopped to look into a shop window, a basic method of observing the reflected street scene and people in the immediate vicinity. Then he relaxed and watched with amusement as the figure moved further along the opposite pavement, stopping every now and then to repeat the crude anti-surveillance precautions. Bruno picked up his paper and immersed himself in the headlined article on the front page. Several minutes later he shook his newspaper and without looking up he said.

"Take a seat Marcel. It's about time you arrived."

The man moved from behind Bruno and took a seat opposite, a slight frown furrowing his brow.

"How did you know it was me?" Marcel asked.

"I've been watching you for the past ten minutes," smiled Bruno. "Remind me to give you some anti-surveillance tips sometime." He glanced behind him to a flower-seller's stall and raising his voice slightly, called, "You can come and join us too, Anton."

There was a deep chuckle and a tall blonde man stepped from behind the floral display and joined Bruno and Marcel at the table. There could not have been a more surprisingly unmatched pair. Marcel and Anton had met while serving with the French Foreign Legion and had become firm friends. Anton looked the typically tall, blue-eyed, pale-skinned, blonde Aryan that the Nazi Party had been so taken with while they had been in power. In contrast, Marcel was a small, swarthy Frenchman of Armenian extraction, who, while not the most tuned instrument in the orchestra, did possess a natural cunning that had often kept him several steps ahead of pursuing gendarmes. A wound during a knife fight had left a scar on his right cheek that pulled his lips up into what seemed to be a permanent sneer.

Bruno ordered coffee and cognac and while they sipped appreciatively, he explained why he had summoned them.

"I have a contract which will pay extremely well, if you are both prepared to commit yourselves to an agreement. There will be a payment of ten thousand pounds to each of you plus any expenses you incur." Pausing, Bruno took a sip of cognac then lowering his voice he continued. "The job concerns the abduction of two children. If you have any reservations about this particular type of work, now is the time to say so."

Bruno looked enquiringly at the two men in turn. Anton pursed his lips and looked sideways at Marcel. Marcel, his eyes gleaming, gave it some thought then nodded his head.

"We have no objections about this type of work," said Anton. "Tell us what you want us to do. We are in."

"Good," smiled Bruno, pushing an envelope across the table. "Welcome aboard. Here are two flight tickets to London and an amount of cash for whatever expenses you will have. When you arrive in London book into a hotel, then phone me, my number is written on the envelope."

Bruno finished his cognac, then standing, shook hands with both men and throwing some francs on to the table he strode away towards the taxi rank, well pleased with the way the meeting had gone.

***

"It looks like we have no alternative but to see how far the cave stretches," Chris remarked, uncertainty in his voice as he bent down and peered into the dark recesses of the tunnel.

"The air in here is quite fresh," observed Mirela, her eyes casting about anxiously. "I've noticed the candle flickering occasionally. There could be an opening at the far end, but if the tunnel becomes too narrow for us to crawl through we could become trapped."

Chris nodded. "Okay – we'll have to chance it, but first we have to make sure that the dogs can't follow us."

With Mirela's help, Chris rolled up the three sleeping bags into a tight bundle, then using a rope to tie them together, he left enough to pass through the centre of the bundle and leave a length trailing.

He stopped often to nurse his injured arm, clenching his teeth against the pain that made him grimace. Mirela collected the torch and with a nod from Chris, led the way into the tunnel, leaving the sounds of the attack on the barricade behind.

Soon they were forced to stoop, then to crawl, as the roof gradually lowered, and the way became narrower. They must have travelled about sixty feet when Chris stopped to rest. Sweating and panting with the effort of dragging the bundle behind him, he gave one last tug on the rope effectively jamming the space behind them. Finding a spur, he tied the rope to it and lay where he was to recover his strength, but as he lay there he felt as if the roof was pressing down on him. He had never liked enclosed places and a worm of fear began to uncoil in his mind. What if they got stuck and couldn't turn back? With an effort he smothered the thought and crawled to where Mirela waited, taking comfort from the light provided by the torch. Trying to control the quaver in his voice he spoke.

"Try only to use the torch when necessary Mirela, we must conserve the batteries as much as we can."

She shone the torch ahead briefly then snapped it off. She too, was battling with her demons. The thought of being buried alive was a constant nagging thought in her mind and her skin crawled at the thought of coming in to contact with creepy crawlies, and worse still, rats. She had already heard the scuttling and squealing up ahead and her mind cringed with revulsion.

They crawled on, apprehension beginning to mount as they felt the roof of the tunnel lower and the sides pressing in. They were down to squirming their way forward, arms stretched out ahead of them and toes gripping the floor, pushing forward an inch at a time. Chris felt the panic begin to rise and could hear his own heartbeat pounding in his ears. His breath came in gasps as he fought to stay in control. His hand touched Mirela's foot and he grasped her ankle, desperately needing the reassurance of her presence as he fought the darkness in his mind. Her voice came floating back to him, shrill and shaking, on the verge of hysteria. Cobwebs were clinging to her face and hair and something had run across the nape of her neck and beneath the collar of her dress. Instinctively, she rubbed her back against the roof and felt something squash inside her dress. She shuddered with revulsion, her spirit weakening so she was almost ready to admit defeat.

"The tunnel's too narrow – we can't go any further. Oh! Chris – we're trapped."

Chris, gathering his wits, took a deep breath and shook Mirela's foot.

"Switch the torch on Mirela and see what's up ahead." A faint glow appeared. Chris was shocked at how impossibly enclosed Mirela's body was within the rock. There was hardly room for the light to filter through from up ahead.

"What do you see Mirela?" He called hoarsely.

"I – I think the tunnel could be widening. It bears to the right and it looks a little wider," she called back with a note of hope in her voice.

Chris let go of Mirela's foot as she began to squirm forward once more. He followed her, his shoulders scraping painfully against the sides of the tunnel. He forced his body to respond to the need to escape the coffin like confines of the shaft, surging forward with every effort of his exhausted body, ignoring his skinned hands and elbows and the burning wound to his arm.

Gradually, the pressure of the shaft lessened as they writhed their way around the bend until Mirela stopped to rest and switched on the torch again. Chris heard her gasp suddenly.

"Oh! No!" she groaned softly, then fell silent.

"What is it Mirela? What's there?" Chris cried, with apprehension.

He heard a muffled sob then her choked, barely audible reply.

"It's a dead end – we can't go any further, there's just a rock face."

He closed his eyes and laid his head on his arm. The fragile hope he had nurtured minutes ago ebbed away to be replaced by the crushing weight of hopelessness that drained his strength and brought hot tears to his eyes.

To Mirela, they seemed to have lay there silent and unmoving in the darkness for a long time. What could they do? It would be very difficult, if not impossible, to try and crawl all the way back to the main cave. Would they have the strength? And even if they made it, there was sure to be someone waiting for them. As Mirela mulled these thoughts over in her mind, there was a trickle of something, a fleeting thought she was unable to grasp, nagging to catch her attention. She lay, not thinking, trying to invite the sliver of thought to reveal itself. Then she felt a wisp of hair flutter delicately across her brow and felt the ever so slight caress of a draught brush the still wet tears on her cheeks.

Gradually it dawned on her – if there was a flow of air there had to be an opening. She switched on the torch and played it over the rock face ahead. There was still the dead end that barred their way, but when she held the torch at a certain angle there seemed to be a crease on the left-hand wall that caused a dim shadow. Pulling herself closer, the shadow gradually widened, until closer still, she found herself staring into an opening in the rock, a sharp left-hand angle that was the continuance of the main tunnel.

Her heart thumping with relief and anticipation, she called excitedly for Chris to join her. His elation that they had discovered a way out was plain when he called back. It would be tricky because they would have to fold themselves around the rock to enter the new angle. Mirela struggled briefly only when her hips became stuck, then she was through and called back that the tunnel was much wider at her end and that it also led downward. Chris had more of a struggle getting his chest and shoulders through the opening and was quite exhausted when at last he was able to re-join Mirela.

After a brief rest and with renewed energy they continued to crawl until the roof heightened and they were able to walk in a stooped position. Their spirits were soaring by the time they reached the exit to the tunnel and they found themselves standing on a wide ledge that led into a large grotto.

The light from the torch revealed quite a large cavern adorned with an array of stalactite and stalagmite rock formations that must have taken many years to build up. The cavern stretched away beyond the beam of the torch. Below their feet a still, dark pool barred their way forward. However, when Mirela shone the torch to the right they could see a narrow ledge jutting out of the rock face, skirting the pool that would take them towards dry ground, and what looked like the entrance to another tunnel that would perhaps allow them to escape this subterranean world. They clambered up on to the ledge that was barely wide enough for their feet and shuffled awkwardly forward, clinging precariously to the rock wall, stopping often to flash the torch onto the ledge ahead to make sure that there were no unseen obstacles that would make them stumble and fall into the cold, dark waters below.

They were almost half way around the pool when Chris reached out and grasped Mirela's hand. He put his lips close to her ear and whispered.

"Listen."

There, behind them, she could hear a slight scrabbling sound coming from the tunnel they had just left. The sound was coming nearer then they heard the sound of loud panting as the creature emerged from the tunnel. Chris squeezed Mirela's hand and they both remained silent as they hugged the rough surface of the rock. Somehow, their pursuers had been able to unblock the tunnel and send one of the dogs after them. They could hear it snuffling around in the dark and then there was a deep-throated growl as it found their scent and began to bark furiously in their direction. Chris, nearest to the tunnel exit, took the torch and shone it on the dog. It presented a frightening sight as it stood on its hind legs, slavering and snarling ferociously, setting up a racket that echoed around the chamber and bounced off the walls in a most unnerving way.

"We are safe here Mirela, it can't reach us," Chris said reassuringly. "Let's move on and reach the dry area as quickly as we can. I don't think there will be anyone following the dog. It was a tight enough squeeze for us, an adult would never make it."

With relief they reached the other side of the pool and entered the new tunnel, leaving the dog's din behind them. It was a much larger shaft, so it enabled them to walk the rest of the distance upright. They reached the exit after travelling about seventy-five metres. They sank down to rest and to decide their next step. The way out was covered by dense undergrowth that allowed only filtered light to enter the place where they sat.

Chris put his arm around Mirela and hugged her to him.

"I didn't think we were going to make it for a while back there," he said grimly.

"Me neither," Mirela confessed, returning his hug.

"You did pretty well – for a girl that is," Chris said, grinning.

"Good of you to say so," answered Mirela, looking at him pertly. "You look awful."

"Yes – I guess we're both in a sorry state," he said, pursing his lips.

They were silent for a while until Mirela said reflectively.

"Why do you think they sent the dog after us? It would have attacked us if it had caught up with us."

"Yes – that worries me," fretted Chris. "Perhaps it was a mistake. Or perhaps they wanted to force us out into the open where they could catch us more easily."

"So, they could be patrolling the area waiting for us to pop up?" mused Mirela.

"Let's take a look," decided Chris, standing up and pushing back the undergrowth. "We can't stay here forever."

Leaving their hiding place, they noted where the entrance was and carefully made their way to the edge of a small adjacent wood. They peered through the shrubbery as they moved around the perimeter of the wood, taking care not to show themselves. They decided to stay at one viewpoint because below them was a lane and if their pursuers were using vehicles, they would use a road such as this. They stayed in that spot some time, enjoying the feel of the warm sunlight filtering through the canopy above them, the sweet smell of grass and foliage and the musty smell of fertile earth.

The sudden sound of a car engine broke their reverie and they watched as a vehicle carrying several men and a number of dogs passed below where they lay. The car stopped at a crossroads a short distance away and two men with dogs got out and then the car drove on. Chris jumped to his feet and called softly to Mirela as he started to make his way back to the hideout. When she didn't answer he turned back to find her sitting cross-legged with her back against a tree and her eyes closed. He reached out a hand to touch her, but he changed his mind, knowing from past experience that he must give her time when she entered a trance-like state. He glanced worriedly down at the road, but the men had disappeared. He ventured out of the trees to look for them and saw them making their way along a lane that ran parallel with the wood.

Returning to where he had left Mirela, he found her waiting for him and together they hastened back to the tunnel where they knew they would be reasonably safe. They discussed their situation and agreed to wait until dark before attempting to reach the farm. They knew they stood more chance of slipping past any groups still looking for them under the cloak of darkness.

"Can you tell me what you were doing when you went into that meditative state while we were in the wood?" Chris asked curiously.

"I was trying to contact my grandmother, but I don't think my ability is strong enough yet over distances," said Mirela pensively. "Grandmother, on the other hand, has extraordinary psychic abilities and it's possible she may have picked up a thread of my message. I'm sure she'll be aware of what's happening and will be searching for us."

Chris, fascinated by the subject, wondered how much greater Mirela's abilities would increase over time. What powers would she have when she was a mature woman?

"Grandmother thinks I will be more gifted than she is. But I don't know – we will just have to wait and see," she explained.

They were silent for a while, both lost in their own thoughts. When Mirela began to fidget, Chris looked at her and raised his eyebrows questioningly.

"What is the information you have that is so important to the people who want to capture you?" She asked, stopping her fidgeting and looking directly at Chris.

"I really don't know," he murmured. "Perhaps they think I know where my parents are."

Mirela pondered his answer and again sensed that he was keeping something back. Something he was either unwilling, or afraid, to tell her. She was about to question him further when they heard a slight rustling in the undergrowth that hid the entrance to the tunnel. They both tensed, ready to flee should their pursuers again appear. They waited with baited breath, ears straining to catch the smallest sound. The rustling came again, nearer this time. Chris leapt to his feet beckoning urgently for Mirela to follow him, but she remained where she was, listening intently. Then she smiled. "It's all right, Chris, it's only my grandmother," she explained. "She must have got my message."

Rosanna stepped into the gloom of the tunnel entrance and her heart fluttered with concern when she saw the condition of the two children. Their dirt-smudged, tear-stained, fragile-looking faces, white smudges in the dimness. Their torn clothes, skinned elbows and bloodied knees, a testament to the hardships they had endured during their escape. Hugging the children to her she was aghast at the injury Chris had sustained to his arm. After questioning him she realized it was essential to get him to hospital as soon as possible so he could have his wound dressed and have an anti-tetanus injection.

"Come children, Sam is nearby, he will take us away from here. We can't risk going back to the farm, so we will visit friends of mine who will give us shelter."

Chapter Seven

It was starting to get light when they eventually reached their destination. The Gypsy camp was situated beside the River Ithon, near to the village of Dolau, an area of natural beauty with rolling hills and lush valleys, a place that Rosanna remembered well from her younger days when she had travelled the circuit with her Gypsy family.

Having packed clothing for the children for just such an emergency, they had stayed at her friend's farm for several hours to allow Mirela and Chris to bathe, to have a change of clothing and have something to eat before they continued their journey. Rosanna had taken precautions to have Chris treated at a hospital some distance from the area that they had fled, in the hope that if any checks were made to try to find the children, their pursuers would not think of casting their net as wide as the town that they had visited. The journey had taken many hours and the children had slept some of the way, but now they were wide-eyed and curious as they stepped from the car to survey their new home.

There was already some activity around the camp-fire that was central to a collection of gaily-painted caravans. When they approached the fire, they were greeted with kindness, offered a hot drink and encouraged to sit beside the fire to warm themselves.

Mirela, with her inherited appearance, blended quite naturally with the people gathered there, but Chris became quite self-conscious when he found he was the centre of attention. His blonde hair and blue eyes provoked such curiosity that when they approached to touch his hair, he retreated back into the car. Moments later Sam and Rosanna appeared and when Sam climbed into the car and started the engine, Rosanna beckoned for Chris to come with her.

"We must do something about your appearance, Chris," she declared, with a sympathetic smile. "Otherwise we won't be able to hide you so effectively."

Chris had already noted that earrings seemed to be standard adornment for both male and female members of the band.

"I'm not wearing earrings," he said, adamantly. "I'll just feel silly in them."

"What was that young man?" A deep voice grated, close by.

Chris spun round and gazed up in dismay at the tallest man he had ever seen glaring down at him. He looked immense in his pantaloons, thick stockings and buckled boots; a loose white shirt was worn beneath a leather jerkin and a black bandanna covered his head, and of course, he sported a pair of gold earrings. The giant cocked his head, waiting for an answer.

"Well – er – perhaps just one then," gulped Chris.

"And pray, where would you like to wear this earring?" asked the giant. "In your nose, on your tongue, or in your belly button?"

Chris, undecided how he should answer, smiled timidly up at his inquisitor. The fearsome eyes beneath beetled eyebrows suddenly softened and the giant threw his head back and roared with laughter.

"Take him away Rosanna," he boomed. "I don't want to recognise him next time I see him."

Mirela sauntered from the caravan where she was to stay with her grandmother. She had changed into clothes that would be more in-keeping with what the women folk of the tribe usually wore, liking the short-sleeved blouse, the sleeveless tunic and the long, colourful loose skirt that reached to her ankles.

Seeing a small figure sitting on the steps of one of the caravans, she changed direction and moved towards the figure with intention of becoming acquainted. As she neared the boy he raised his head and stared at her. Her eyes widened in surprise when she found she was staring at Chris. She would not have recognized him had it not been for his brilliant blue eyes. He had changed totally and was plainly not pleased about it. His hair was now a dark brown colour and his face had taken on a swarthy tawny complexion that emphasised the colour of his eyes even more. He too had changed into attire normally worn by the boys who were present in the camp.

"You look – different," smiled Mirela, raising a hand to her mouth to stifle the giggle that threatened to burst out when she saw the glint of an earring in Chris's right ear.

"Your grandmother is a very persuasive person," he said tightly, glaring at Mirela. "Especially when that giant of a man is lurking about watching everything that is going on."

"That's Ruben, the clan Chieftain. His word is law to everyone, and to us too," cautioned Mirela. "Come, let's explore the camp and get to know the people, we could be here for some time."

As they walked together, Mirela asked, "I can understand that they used a dye for your hair, but how did they change the colour of your skin?"

"Berries – they crushed berries and used the juice to stain my face and hands," said Chris, with disgust. "Your grandmother said there wasn't much she could do to hide the colour of my eyes, other than for me to wear dark glasses."

"That should complete the transformation," teased Mirela, linking her arm through his and smiling mischievously.

Despite his feelings of displeasure, Chris found himself chuckling in response to Mirela's humour and soon his mood brightened as she led him to mingle with others that were gathered around the camp-fire.

***

The days went slipping by and soon it was time for the tribe to move on to a new location. In the time it had taken the children to adjust to their new life they had experienced many of the ways of the Gypsy, and their association with the Gadje. Gadje (foreigner) was the name given to people who were not Romany. Mirela and her grandmother joined the women in visiting nearby towns and villages to sell their wares.

Flowers, pegs and woven willow baskets were sold from door to door and occasionally fortunes told, and palms read for an extra coin or two.

Mirela learned much as she watched her grandmother reveal the skilled approach she used in dealing with the Gadje. She used a mixture of persuasion and humour learnt in her earlier life on the road but became solemn when asked to read a palm or tell a fortune, for with her gift, she was able to see much more than most fortune tellers. Very occasionally, she would press the coin back into the person's palm and close their hand with the excuse that she was unable to read the signs because the palm was clouded and inscrutable, then taking Mirela's hand they would hurry away.

Mystified, Mirela asked, "Why were you not able to read that person's palm, grandmother?"

"Sometimes the markings show too much future unhappiness and very little joy," explained Rosanna. "If I cannot tell of these things then I will not take their coin. In time, you too will be confronted by this dilemma."

Mirela would have liked to have practised her palmistry but realized she would have to be patient for she was really too young for the Gadje to take seriously.

Chris accompanied the men when they too went calling at houses in the local communities and was persuaded to push the colourful cart that carried the stone for sharpening knives and tools. Gradually, Ruben took him under his wing and began to teach him about the grys (horses). Chris, a willing pupil, found Ruben to be a firm but fair tutor with a teasing sense of humour. Chris's respect and liking for him grew with each day and he became impatient when other chores kept him away from Ruben and the horses. He worked hard at learning about the many herbs and remedies, gathered from the countryside, that were used to treat the various ailments that the horses would suffer from. He learnt how to diagnose illnesses by looking into the horse's mouth, examining its eyes, feeling its fetlocks, stroking and prodding its body and probing its hooves.

Farmers, knowing the Gypsy way with horses, would invite Ruben or one of the men to visit their farm to look at an ailing horse. More often than not, they would be able to treat the animal and bring it back to health, thereby pleasing the farmer who would pay quite willingly for the treatment and would often purchase the herbal medication that the Gypsies had used.

Village fetes and horse fairs were always popular with the Gypsies. It was a time when most of the tribe got involved in doing something, be it horse-trading, telling fortunes, playing a musical instrument, dancing, or simply involved in selling wares. Chris, very much involved with those who would do the horse-trading, would ride to the fair upon one of the horses and be responsible for the feeding and watering of the stock. Haggling would be fierce and when a sale was struck both parties would seal the sale by spitting on their palm and shaking hands.

When the music started Chris would sneak away to watch the dancing, but he was never really successful in leaving without being noticed. As always, he and Mirela couldn't make a move without being watched by at least one or more of the tribe. He enjoyed watching Mirela as she whirled and swayed and stamped her feet in time to the music, bringing cries of admiration from the musicians and loud applause from the gathered crowd. He had often watched Rosanna instructing Mirela in the practice of some intricate steps and the correct way to strike a pose. Intrigued by the dancing, Chris asked Ruben about it.

"It's a type of flamenco dance that originated in Spain," explained Ruben. "A very dramatic and tempestuous way of interpreting the courtship between a man and a woman, it can be danced by couples or by a single person. We Romany took it and gave it our own interpretation and it is danced as you see it now."

Chris had so many questions he wanted to ask about the Romany. He decided to chance asking them while he recognized Ruben was in a benign and talkative mood.

"Where do the Romany come from, Ruben?"

Ruben studied Chris for a moment and then said, "Nowhere and everywhere. We are the persecuted of many lands. We travel because we are acceptable to the Gadje only while we travel, and it has become a way of life for many generations of Romany. It is unthinkable for us to live any other way." He paused in thought then said. "Not all men are like trees; some must travel and cannot keep still."

Slowly the tribe made their way through Wales, staying at each location for about four weeks then moving on. The children adapted quickly to their new life and found it exciting to wake up and be involved in the daily routine of the camp. Everyone had the responsibility to complete certain tasks that made the camp run like a well-oiled machine. As soon as all the chores were done, the children knew that the real work of the day would begin.

The women would gather their wares and a horse would be harnessed to one of the vardos (wagons) to take them to the nearest town. The vardo would lead the way and the horses to be sold that day would bring up the rear. The area where they had made camp was near to the village of Bethlehem, close to the foot of the Black mountains. There were a number of villages in the area, so each one could be visited in turn to do door-to-door business with the Gadje. The main town, Llandeilo, was where the horse fair was to be conducted. Chris had become quite used to riding bareback by now and was able to shepherd the other horses into a group, so they didn't stray.

The trading was vigorous and by mid-afternoon all the horses they had brought had been sold and several had been purchased. Chris thought that the horses purchased were in a sorry condition, but he now knew that with care and attention Ruben would make sure that they would be in the best of condition when being sold on at a later fair. Tired, but buoyant with the way business had gone, the troupe made their way back to camp for a well-earned rest, and where they could while away the evening after a satisfying meal.

Nobody noticed the horseman that followed at a safe distance until they reached the campsite, then turning his horse he galloped away at speed with a pleased look on his face. A chill breeze had sprung up during the evening, so many of the company had decided to retire to their vardos. Chris accompanied Rosanna and Mirela to their caravan, and when they were comfortably settled in, Mirela asked her grandmother to show her how to set out the tarot cards. As Rosanna shuffled the cards, Chris asked if she would do a reading for him.

"Not really," she answered. "Children are unformed. They are not adults and at times can be far too imaginative. It has been found that a child could be too influenced by vague references as to what may happen in the future. This could lead to the child being unduly troubled and also bring about behavioural problems."

"But I'm not a child," protested Chris. "I'm almost fifteen. Couldn't we pretend to do a reading just for fun?"

Rosanna continued to shuffle the cards, her brow knitted with indecision, then sighing, she said, "Very well, but the tarot is not a fun thing. It is a very powerful medium that must be taken seriously."

She gave the cards to Chris for him to shuffle and cut as he liked. Then Rosanna took the cards back and selected one from the pack – The Knave – this would be the significator, a pictorial representation of Chris. This she lay on the table face-up. Taking nine cards from the top of the pack, she laid each one face-up to form the shape of a Celtic cross, murmuring in a strange tongue as she did so. She hesitated slightly before taking the tenth card, sliding it slowly from the pack and laying it in place to complete the cross, then staring fixedly at it as though mesmerised. It was The Hermit, dressed in a long flowing habit and leaning on a simple staff, bravely holding his tiny light towards the darkness. The sudden chilling hoot of an owl broke the spell and Rosanna, looking up and shivering slightly, reached out to gather up the cards. Chris, mystified by Rosanna's reaction, laid his hands on the remaining cards and asked, questioningly.

"What can you tell me Rosanna? What did you read?"

"Nothing, I read nothing. I can draw no conclusion because the cards fell in a meaningless pattern. Perhaps we can try another day."

She gathered up the rest of the cards and put them away, then pulling a shawl around her she hurried down the steps and made her way towards another caravan. Chris watched her go and looked searchingly at Mirela.

"I don't know," she shrugged. "Perhaps it was the owl that upset her. We Romany are a very superstitious lot. An owl hooting nearby is not usually viewed as a good omen."

Chris, not entirely convinced that this was the explanation, remained silent. He had great respect for Rosanna and Mirela and for the apparent special gift that they both shared, but it could be frustrating when they decided that it was better for him not to know certain things that clearly concerned him.

Chapter Eight

The phone rang in Bruno Fletcher's apartment just as he was about to leave. Lifting the receiver, he answered irritably.

"Yes."

"Is that Mr Bruno Fletcher?"

"That rather depends upon who's calling. I suggest you identify yourself," he said testily.

"You won't know me because we have never met," said the voice in an unmistakeable Welsh accent. "But I have some information that will be of great importance to you."

"Okay, spit it out."

"Not so fast, my friend. The information I have is going to cost you."

"Look, don't waste my time," snarled Bruno. "How would you know what kind of information I want?"

"I know because my company was hired to do the same job that you have been hired to do," said the voice, knowingly. "Unfortunately, our strategy didn't work so we lost the contract."

"Oh yes – and what kind of contract was that?"

"The contract involved finding a boy and handing him over to a certain party. But now it seems that a girl is involved, and you have to find her too."

"What makes you think that we don't already know where these children are?"

The voice chuckled, sardonically.

"If you knew where they were, you would already have made an attempt to take them."

Bruno chewed his lip as he considered his options. He was aware that others had been hired to find the children before him, and they had been unsuccessful. The children had disappeared into thin air and no matter where he had searched he had come up empty handed. His employers were impatient for results and if he didn't find them soon he too would lose the contract.

"What's your price?" asked Bruno.

"Twenty thousand pounds. To be placed in a numbered account in a bank of my choice."

"You must be out of your mind if you think I will pay you that kind of money," spluttered Bruno, angrily.

"Take it, or leave it," said the voice. "But I am also willing to watch them and report their whereabouts to you until you are ready to act."

"With the resources I can call upon, I will find them," stated Bruno. "However, if your information proves useful I will pay you five thousand pounds cash, then if we succeed in taking the children, I will place ten thousand pounds into a numbered account of your choice. You must also agree to work with my men when they deliver the money to you. Now, where can I reach you?"

The voice on the other end of the phone was silent for a moment. Then, recognizing that Bruno was probably an expert negotiator, and perhaps this could lead to being hired again sometime in the future, grudgingly, the sum was accepted, and a meeting place was arranged. Bruno, cautiously positive and satisfied with the way he had dealt with the Welshman, immediately made a call to Anton and Marcel to tell them that he had recruited another person, a

Welshman who had important information, and told them where to find him, instructing them to report back as soon as they had this information.

Bruno sat pondering the news he had received from Anton. *So, that was where the children were hidden, with travelling Gypsies. How clever! If it hadn't been for the Welshman, they may have remained hidden indefinitely. This time there must be no mistakes. I must plan carefully.* He thought deeply for more than an hour, hardly stirring, then he picked up the receiver dialled a number and asked to speak to Marcel.

"Marcel, what do you know about travelling Gypsies? Really, your grandparents were Gypsies? That's fortunate. Then you should know something about their culture."

Bruno listened to Marcel for a few moments then interrupted him.

"Yes – yes, I know you slipped up when you accidentally released the dog to follow the children along the tunnel. Fortunately, they must have been out of reach of the dog, or there could have been serious repercussions if the creature had caught up with them and they had been savaged. I want no mistakes this time – now here is what I want you to do…"

Chapter Nine

Life went on as usual in the camp. Chris and Mirela, although they loved the countryside and would occasionally wander off to explore a nearby stream or wood, knew not to stray too far out of sight of the sentinels who had been assigned to watch over them.

There was a visitor to the tribe. His name was Michel and he was a French Gypsy who had approached Ruben at the last horse fair, asking if he could stay with the tribe for a while. He was small and swarthy, with a thatch of curly black hair that almost hid the gold earrings that he wore in each ear. A set of white teeth that flashed whenever he smiled and a scar on his right cheek completed the roguish appearance of the newcomer. It seemed that, for one reason or another, he had decided to come to Britain in the hope that he would be accepted into the British Romany culture and perhaps be granted a place in a tribe. Gypsy tradition declared that the Chieftain could give his consent for a person to join the tribe as long as that person followed the tribal laws, blended in with the people and proved to be industrious in the daily activities of the camp.

Michel had enthusiastically joined in with the festivities at the horse fair and had entertained everyone with his dramatic interpretation of the Spanish *pasodoble* dance, commenting afterwards that it was much better danced with a lady partner. Later, he had returned to camp with the group and been given a space where he could park his vardo.

Several days later, early one morning, Chris and Mirela noticed Michel returning to camp in his vardo. He hailed them and when he had drawn near he asked if they would like some freshly caught fish, explaining in his thickly accented voice that he was good at tickling trout, and that he took his vardo out to the river in the evening so that he could rise early and be on the riverbank when the fish were feeding near the surface.

He placed three fat trout into Mirela's hands, saying he had more than enough for his own needs and that they were quite welcome to the surplus catch. Mirela, ever suspicious of people whom she didn't know, would have refused the gift of the fish, but when she looked askance at Chris he just shrugged non-committaly.

"I come from the Camargue, in the south of France," said Michel proudly. "Where I was taught early in my childhood how to catch fish. I was also taught how to dance the *pasodoble,* which you probably saw me perform at the horse fair. It is a dance that replicates the gestures and manoeuvres of the Matador during a bullfight. To dance the *pasodoble* properly, it is better to have a lady partner who acts as the Matador's cape."

Mirela shuddered slightly. "I think bullfighting is one of the cruellest sports in the world," she declared. "How so many people can enjoy that kind of thing is awful."

"Not all bullfights are brutal," commented Michel. "The Camargue has a bull game whereby men dressed in white try to grab the ribbon that is placed between the bull's horns. Sometimes the men are injured, but never the bull."

"That sounds like fun to watch," smiled Mirela. "And much more civilized."

"I saw you dance the flamenco while at the horse fair. I thought you were very good," Michel said, looking quizzically at Mirela. "If you would like to learn the *pasodoble* I would be willing to instruct you and perhaps it would add to the entertainment at a future fair."

Mirela hesitated. Instinctively, her awareness heightened, and she could see Michel's aura. At the centre it was a deep, passionate red that paled and fused into a lighter yellow, then became a pastel green, which blurred at the fringes. The blurring could denote several things, an illness, a bad experience, or a flaw in one's nature. She was unsure of how to react to Michel's offer, so she took the female prerogative of giving the demure.

"Perhaps."

Chris, who had been silent until now, intrigued by the thought of being able to catch fish in such a simple way, asked, "Will you take us fishing with you some time and show us how you tickle fish?"

"Of course, I will let you know when I will be going again."

Michel climbed back up on his vardo and waving to the children drove off to present fish to other fortunate members of the band.

There was to be a wedding. This news was greeted with great excitement, as arrangements for the ceremony were made and abundant food and drink was prepared for the many people who would be attending. Mirela, after several sessions of instruction from Michel, always observed closely by Rosanna, was now able to dance the *pasodoble*. Indeed, Michel was much impressed by how quickly she had learnt the intricate steps and the dramatic movements that so personified the drama of the Corrida. It was planned that they would dance the *pasodoble* at the wedding and dedicate it to the happy couple.

The wedding, called the *abiav*, came about on a warm summer's day. There was feverish activity until it was time for the whole tribe to gather for the formalities to begin. Ruben presided over the traditional, but simple ceremony. The bride and groom joined hands and promised to be true to each other, then sitting, surrounded by relatives and friends, a small amount of salt and bread was placed on the knees of the bride. The groom took some of the bread, put salt on it and ate it. The bride did the same. The union of salt and bread symbolized a harmonious future for the happy couple.

Soon the festivities began. A whole pig, a side of beef and chickens, cooked on spits over open fires and soon wafted enticing smells about the camp. Musicians tuned up their instruments and drinks were dispensed to toast the bride and groom. This was the children's first experience of a Romany wedding and they were swept along by the joy and excitement of it all. There was such a festive atmosphere that everyone, no matter what they were engaged in, seemed to have a smile on their face.

The band struck up and soon couples began to dance. The laughter and gaiety were so infectious that Mirela even encouraged Chris to join her in a simple Gypsy jig. At last the moment came for Mirela and Michel to take to the arena for their exhibition dance. Mirela wore a long, scarlet dress and Michel had on a bright yellow, puffed-sleeved shirt and dark trousers, demonstrating in a simple way the *torero*. A trumpet sounded the entrance call, as was customary during the Corrida, and Mirela and Michel took their places to begin the dance. The whole camp had come to watch and as the *pasodoble* began the onlookers clapped in time to the music. Mirela and Michel strutted, whirled and swayed, in time to the music, backs arched, and heads held high as Michel flung Mirela out then drew her back again, interpreting the matador's sweeping gestures with the cape. The finale came with Mirela, sprawled on the ground as the bullfighter discards the cape, and Michel falling to his knees as the dance comes to an end. The applause and cries of appreciation from their audience were loud and long as Mirela and Michel took their bow, then walked in a proud and stately fashion from the arena.

***

Mirela had awakened early. She met a yawning and sleepy-eyed Chris and walked with him towards Michel's caravan, their shoes becoming soaked as they made their way through the dew-drenched grass. There were very few people about at that time of morning as most were sleeping off the celebratory excesses of the previous day. The celebrations could continue for a further day if the bride and groom's families so decided.

Michel had approached them the previous evening informing them that he was going fishing the next morning, and if they wanted to go with him they must be ready to leave at six a.m. Chris had found the men who were to be on sentinel duty the next day and had notified them that he and Mirela intended to leave the camp early the next morning to go fishing with Michel. In a jolly, drink-induced mood, they had promised to meet him at the allotted time, but added, if they didn't turn up he was to call them.

When Chris and Mirela arrived, Michel had already harnessed the horse to the caravan and sat holding the reins ready to go.

"Right! Climb up and we will be on our way," called Michel impatiently.

"The sentinels were supposed to meet us here," said Chris, looking around. "We can't go without them, Ruben would be furious. It looks like they have overslept, I'll have to go and give them a call."

"Very well — if you must, but hurry, the fish won't stay near the surface all morning," advised Michel, barely curbing his impatience.

Chris hurried away toward a group of caravans and returned some ten minutes later leading a young man who looked much the worse for wear.

"It doesn't look as if his partner will make it," said Chris with disgust. "He just mumbled something and turned over."

Soon they were on their way with Chris and Mirela perched alongside Michel on the driver's seat and the young sentinel resting inside the vardo. Reaching a shaded spot, they settled on the bank of the river and Michel began to show Chris how to tickle the fish into immobility before scooping them out of the water and onto the bank. Although Chris tried hard to emulate Michel's technique, he failed to catch any fish at all, while Michel seemed to scoop them out with ease.

"Practice and patience, young man," said Michel, with a knowing look. "Practice and patience."

They decided to take a rest and joined Mirela who was sitting beneath a tree immersed in a book. The sentinel lay stretched out nearby, dealing with his hangover. When Michel produced a bottle of lemonade the sentinel drank deeply of the refreshing liquid then passed it to Chris who also drank thirstily. Michel poured a quantity into a cup for Mirela that she sipped sparingly.

"Drink up Mirela, I have several more bottles tucked away so you can drink as much as you like," said Michel, generously.

Knowing the importance of drinking enough fluids during warm weather, she responded by finishing the contents of the cup. Suddenly, she was aware that Chris was struggling to stand up. He looked at her, trying to keep his eyes open and to bring her into focus, his lips trying to form words but failing. Unable to communicate with her he slumped back, closed his eyes and lay still. Near to Chris the sentinel was laying on his side, his legs moving as in slow motion and his hands scrabbling at the earth in a futile effort to rise. She looked at Michel in wide-eyed horror, realizing that the drink they had been given had been laced with something to knock them out. She sprang to her feet to flee, but after several steps her head seemed to become too heavy to hold up and the strength left her body, her legs crumpled, and she would have pitched into the river had Michel not caught hold of her.

Quickly, he lifted Mirela and carried her to the caravan, then went back for Chris placing him next to her. An anxious glance over his shoulder at the supine sentinel assured him that there would be no trouble from that direction. Climbing into the driving seat he snapped the reins and set the horse off at a fast pace towards the gate that led to the open road. Using his whip, Michel urged the horse into a gallop. Half a mile further on he stopped briefly to visit a small cottage that looked down onto the road. A face appeared at an upstairs window after he had pounded on the door for several minutes. The door opened to reveal the Welshman, the latest addition to the gang, looking bleary-eyed and still half asleep.

"Why are you still in bed?" questioned Michel, with annoyance. "You are supposed to be watching for me at this time of morning – never mind – tell the others that I have the children and I will be waiting at the crossroads for them," he said quickly. "Tell them to hurry before the children are missed."

The Welshman snapped alert and after sheepishly acknowledging Michel's message he hurried to the phone.

Chapter Ten

Slack tried to close out the nagging thoughts that prevented him from going back to sleep. He gave up and sat up, his head aching abominably. He felt awful and cursed himself for drinking far too much the previous night. He knew he had to make a move or risk Ruben's wrath when he found out that he had shirked his sentinel duty. He dressed hurriedly and staggering down the caravan steps made his way to where Michel would have parked his vardo. Finding the space empty, he followed the wheel tracks towards the river. Arriving at the place where the vardo had stopped, he looked around for signs of life. The only sound was the rustling of trees and the swirl of water as it swept around protruding rocks and flowed onward around the bend. He was about to continue following the tracks when he noticed a form lying on the bank amongst the trees. With trepidation he hurried to the form and turning it over found with a shock that he was staring into the face of his partner who was still in a deeply drugged state. Unable to wake him he sprang up and ran to where the tracks continued across the field. Following the tracks, he stopped suddenly realizing that he didn't know how far ahead Michel would be. It would be better to get help, so turning around he raced back to the camp to raise the alarm.

Slack's urgent shouts as he raced around the caravans stirred the camp into action and soon a number of men, astride horses and carrying rifles, were thundering towards the river. Ruben, on the lead horse, pulled Slack up behind him so he could show them which way to go. Reaching the river, they barely glanced at the huddled form of the other sentinel, still lying unstirred on the riverbank, and swept onward through the gate and onto the road that led to the crossroads.

The horses were breathing hard when Ruben and his men saw Michel's vardo stopped near the crossroads. Pounding their horse's flanks with their heels, they urged their steeds to greater effort and charged down on the unsuspecting Michel who was in the act of transferring Chris from his vardo to a car that was parked nearby.

Hearing the pounding of hooves approaching, Michel turned and looked back in alarm, his heart lurching with fright when he saw Ruben, roaring with anger, leading his men in a charge that would be upon him in no time. He hesitated, calculating if he had enough time to make it to the car with his burden, then deciding he didn't, he dumped Chris unceremoniously on to the grass verge and ran towards the vehicle. As he neared the car a rear door swung open for him, but when bullets from the charging horsemen's rifles flew close overhead, he turned and pulling a pistol from his belt he loosed off several shots into the converging pack of riders. One rider swayed and fell from his horse causing the rest of them to pull to a sliding stop. They had not anticipated return fire and as they milled around in confusion one of the horsemen snapped off a shot. The impact of the striking bullet made Michel stagger back against the open door, his hand falling to his side and the pistol slipping from his nerveless fingers as he slumped sideways to lay half in and half out of the car. A pair of hands appeared and hauled him onto the back seat. Immediately the door slammed, and the car started to reverse at an alarming speed. The engine screaming as the car rocketed along the lane and sliding to a jolting stop at the crossroads it spun right and raced off at high speed.

Rosanna sat between the two cots that contained the children, massaging their hands and feet, stoking their hair and encouraging them to wake up. Chris came around first and then Mirela. They were disorientated and confused at first, but after a hot drink and time to collect their thoughts they recovered quite quickly. Rosanna explained what had happened while they had still been drugged and wept with relief to know they had not been harmed and were safe with her once again.

"I'm sorry grandmother," apologized Mirela, tearfully. "I should have taken more care before trusting Michel, but he seemed such a nice person."

"Don't blame yourself child, I too was at fault," said Rosanna grimly. "Although I warned the sentinels to be extra vigilant because I didn't completely trust him, Michel proved to be very clever and almost succeeded with his plan."

Rosanna checked the children over, looking into their eyes, feeling their pulses, examining their mouths and questioning them as to how they felt. Satisfied that there were no lingering after effects of the drugging, she suggested that they visit Ruben. Ruben greeted them warmly and cursed Michel (that infernal little frog) roundly for his treachery. He apologised for the lapse in security and promised that nothing like that would ever happen again while they remained with him and his tribe. He then took them to visit the man who had been shot by Michel. Luckily, the bullet had bounced off a rib then passed through the fleshy part of his upper arm. Although not able to move around and feeling quite sore, the man was in good spirits and was quite visibly moved when Mirela and Chris thanked him for helping to save them from their kidnappers.

That evening, as they sat in their caravan where it was warm and secure, Rosanna explained that it would not be safe to stay at the camp any longer. Somehow, the people hunting them had tracked them down and penetrated their cover.

"I really thought we would be safe here for some time, but they seem to be able to find us where ever we hide."

Rosanna was silent for a while, thinking, then she said, "We daren't use the seaports or the airports, they seem to have eyes everywhere. We will have to use another form of transport to escape their attention. Pack your things so we will be ready to leave quickly. Meanwhile, I will have to contact Sam who will be a part of the arrangements for our journey out of here."

Sam arrived late one evening to be greeted warmly by Rosanna and the children. It was planned that he would stay overnight, and they would depart early the next morning. As they prepared to leave the next morning, Ruben and several members of the tribe approached to say goodbye. Much to everyone's amusement, and Chris's embarrassment, Ruben seized him in a bear hug.

"Come back and visit us again when you can – do you hear?" and with a chuckle he added. "Next time I will promote you to wearing two earrings for your good work with the horses." Placing Chris back on his feet, he stood back saying, "Take care all of you. We will always be here if you should need us."

As the car made its way out of the camp, Rosanna and the children continued to wave until they turned onto the road and lost sight of everyone. It was silent in the car as Sam gathered speed. Everyone was lost in their own thoughts as they felt the regrets of their departure from a life they had become used to and had grown to love.

Their departure from the camp did not go unnoticed by someone else. As they sped past the cottage near to the camp, the Welshman, hearing the approaching car, was able to follow its progress through his binoculars as far as the crossroads and when it had disappeared from view he hurried to the phone to report the sighting. The early morning call awoke Bruno Fletcher who had been hoping for such news.

"They are on the move. The farmhand has collected the grandmother and the two children in his car. They passed the cottage some minutes ago and turned left at the crossroads heading south."

Chapter Eleven

They made their way through the Black Mountains to Aberdare, then onward toward Newport where they would board a ferry across the River Severn to Somerset. All went well until they reached Pontypridd when they noticed a car, a limousine, that seemed to be following them at a discreet distance. Rosanna encouraged Sam to speed up to try to lose it but when Sam increased his speed, the other car increased its speed too.

They came to a sparsely populated area where there was little traffic and the lane they travelled along was unusually straight. Sam glanced in his mirror to check on the car that was following them and saw a black sports saloon approaching fast. He edged over to allow the car to overtake, which it did, but as soon as it was past it suddenly braked to a tyre-screeching stop just ahead of them and slew around, side on, completely blocking the road.

Taken completely by surprise, Sam slammed on his brakes while glancing swiftly into his rear-view mirror. The car that had been following them for the past few miles was coming up fast. Realizing that it was a trap, he looked desperately around for a way to escape, but there was no way around the saloon.

A gate – there was a closed gate that led into a field, but the gap past the saloon was narrow and he would have to barge his way through. Hesitating no longer, Sam slammed the car into reverse and spurted back for about ten yards, then slipping the car into forward gear he stamped on the accelerator and raced toward the gap. Staying clear of the wall on one side, Sam deliberately smashed into the rear of the saloon shunting it out of the way, spilling the passengers who were climbing out, onto the road. Hurtling towards the gate he crashed through it, scattering pieces of wood in all directions. The car lurched into the field flying over the rough, boggy ground at speed. Fifty yards on the car slowed as the wheels churned up the ground, but when Sam engaged the auxiliary four-wheel drive the car surged forward again, putting distance between them and their pursuers. When Sam looked back to see if there was any pursuit, he was relieved to see that the car that had been following them had attempted to cross the field after them, but had got stuck in the mud, and the men from both cars had gathered to try to free it.

Joining a track on the far side of the field, Sam followed it through an open gate and soon found they were driving through a farmyard, scattering chickens and getting perplexed looks from the occupants of the farm, who were going about their daily chores. Gathering their wits about them again, Rosanna and the children heaved a collective sigh of relief for Sam's special driving skills and for being delivered out of danger again.

"Thank you, Sam. You did exceptionally well to get us out of there," said Rosanna, gratefully. "Any damage to your car will be paid for when you return to the farm." Pausing, she said with bewilderment, "I wish I knew where they get their information from. They seem to know our every movement. It's frightening. We have been extremely lucky so far, but if they continue to pursue us I dread to think what could happen."

"I don't think there will be too much to repair," Sam reassured Rosanna. "The bull bars I fitted took most of the impact," he chuckled. "I think I caused enough damage to the saloon to keep it off the road, so that should cut down the odds." Sam was silent for a few moments, deciding, "Let's head straight for the ferry. If we can make it over to Somerset without meeting up with those thugs again, we'll stand a good chance of staying ahead of them."

They arrived at the ferry terminal without mishap and joined the line of cars waiting for the next sailing. They were third in the queue, so they would be off the ferry on the opposite bank relatively quickly. After purchasing a ticket, they sat quietly waiting for the ferry to arrive. Sam kept glancing in his mirror checking the cars that joined the queue, hoping fervently that their pursuers would not anticipate that they would be catching the ferry, but his heart sank when he noticed a car similar to the one that had followed them from Pontypridd join the tail end of the queue.

A tall blonde man stepped out of the car and proceeded to examine each car that he passed as he approached the front of the queue. Pausing at Sam's car he glanced in at Sam and then at Rosanna and the children. His face was hard and expressionless, and his light-blue eyes conveyed a depth of coldness that made Mirela shudder with foreboding. Slowly, he turned and strode back to his car and climbed in.

Sam turned in his seat and saw the apprehension and the fear on the faces of Rosanna and the children.

"I don't know how many cars the ferry can carry, but they may be too far back to make it onto this one," he said, trying to make them feel less frightened. "If they do make it on to this ferry, at least we will be off before them, which will give us a head start."

The ferry filled up quickly and to Sam's disappointment, he saw that the pursuers car was one of the last to be allowed on. Stroking his bristled chin, he tried to think of something that would delay their pursuers. *I wish to hell they would get a puncture,* he thought fiercely. Then suddenly, he had the answer. *Of course – if I can divert their attention for a short while, perhaps Chris can plant something under one of the wheels.* Quickly, he explained his plan to Rosanna and the children. Chris didn't hesitate but agreed with Sam wholeheartedly. He was only too pleased to think that he would be able to take some kind of revenge against the thugs that were making their lives so intolerable. Sam rummaged in his boot and found a piece of wood with several long nails protruding. He had fashioned it as a directional sign to nail to a tree when umpiring during one of the rallies. Instructing Chris to stay low when he crawled between the cars, he gave him the piece of wood to place under the front wheel and made his way to the side of the ferry where he would be in full view of their pursuers.

Taking out a notebook and pen, Sam pretended to make notes while glancing at the pursuers' car. He knew he had their full attention when all the occupants leaned forward, peering through the windscreen at him. Chris crawled slowly and carefully between the cars until he reached the front of the pursuers' car and jammed the piece of wood, with the nails protruding, under the nearest wheel. He was just about to crawl away when the rear door opened, and someone stepped out onto the deck. Panicking, he scrambled under the front of the car and lay still, hardly breathing. A pair of muddied black shoes and trouser bottoms appeared and stopped for a few moments, then moved away. Chris peered around the wheel and saw that the person who had stepped out onto the deck had moved to the other side of the car, with the obvious intention of trying to intimidate Sam with his presence. Quickly, Chris crawled out from under the car and made his way back to where Rosanna and Mirela were anxiously waiting for him. Noticing Chris was back safely, Sam closed his notebook and giving the thug a perfunctory glance, strolled unhurriedly back to his car.

When the ferry docked they drove off the ramp without a backward glance, happy in the knowledge that if their ploy was not discovered, they would be able to put quite a few miles between them and their pursuers.

Sam stuck to the coast road through Somerset then cut inland when he reached Devon and travelled across Exmoor. They made good time and although keeping a constant watch for any vehicle tailing them, they reached the outskirts of the village of Braunton without mishap. Rosanna directed Sam through a gate toward a collection of farm buildings and outhouses where they stopped and to everyone's relief, alighted to stretch the stiffness out of their limbs after such a long journey. Noticing their arrival, the farmer approached to greet Rosanna warmly and ushered them towards the farmhouse where a meal was being prepared. As they entered the kitchen, the enticing aroma of hotpot and freshly-baked bread made each one of them realize how hungry they were.

After a satisfying meal, the farmer took Rosanna aside and spoke to her.

"Good to see you after such a long time, Rosanna, you look well. How is brother David? Is he still talking about retiring from the farming business?"

"Yes! He still talks of giving everything up and travelling the world," chuckled Rosanna. "But I doubt if he will. What would he do after he has travelled the world? No! He loves farming too much, Joseph, to give it up."

"What is this trouble you mentioned in your letter, and what have the children got to do with it?"

Rosanna explained to Joseph, her brother-in-law, the dreadful situation that the children faced, especially Chris, and why she needed to meet with the man who flew hot air balloons from Joseph's farm.

"We need to fly to the Channel Isles without leaving a trail that can be followed. We can't use the seaports or the airports because they are being watched and they seem to have a way of gaining information about us that I just can't fathom."

Joseph was tall, broad shouldered and athletic looking. Intelligent blue eyes looked out from a rugged, tanned face. Swept back dark hair, greying at the sides, completed the strong, physical characteristics of a purposeful person. His face was grim when he heard Rosanna's explanation.

"What kind of people hunt children in this way?" he said, frowning. "The stakes must be high for them to be so persistent." He thought for a moment then said. "Andrew Chambers is due at the farm tomorrow to do some maintenance on his balloon. You can speak to him then about your wishes. Meanwhile, you all look bushed. Come, I'll show you to your rooms."

Sam declined the offer to stay the night, saying there was much to do at the farm and that he should get back as soon as possible. Rosanna protested that he should stay the night and leave early the next morning, but Sam argued that he should leave under cover of darkness, that way there was less chance of being spotted by those who were looking for them. Rosanna accepted the wisdom of what Sam said and hugging him, thanked him for being their saviour once again, as did the children.

"All part of the service," he said, with a wry smile, and waving nonchalantly, he roared off into the distance.

***

Bruno Fletcher was in a foul mood. He kicked furiously at the punctured wheel, beside himself with anger at being delayed by such a simple trick. They pushed the car off the ferry and quickly changed the wheel. Setting off in pursuit again, Bruno drove the car as fast as it would go, trying to make up for lost time, but he knew that the car they were chasing was faster and unless something happened to delay it, they had little chance of catching it up. He cursed Sam roundly under his breath for putting his fastest car off the road. *I'll save something special for him when I catch up with him,* Bruno promised himself.

Bruno and his men were parked up in the car park of a transport café on the outskirts of Minehead where they had taken a short meal break. He was more optimistic of finding his quarry now that they had had a lucky sighting of the car they had been pursuing. They had stopped in a lay-by while Bruno studied a map of the area when the unmistakable form of the car had appeared out of the gloom, emerging from a minor road a short distance ahead to join the main road travelling back in the opposite direction. The farm hand had been alone in the car, so it was obvious that he had dropped his passengers off somewhere ahead.

Bruno had used the phone at the café to dial the special number he used to obtain information. He had been informed that the grandmother had a brother-in-law, a certain Joseph Dudley, who had a farm in north Devon, close to Ilfracombe. So, this would probably be the place where they were now hiding.

Chapter Twelve

Refreshed after a good night's rest, Rosanna, Chris and Mirela were taken to the barn by Joseph where they were introduced to Andrew Chambers. He was in the process of hauling a trailer, attached to his truck, out of the wide barn doors and into a nearby field. When Rosanna asked Andrew if he would be willing to transport them to the Channel Islands he looked bemused.

"Joseph has told me of your situation and your urgent need to leave the country. But you see, most of the flights that I do are experimental, and I am only licensed to carry one passenger." He bent to untie one of the ropes that held his equipment secured to the trailer, then seeing how crestfallen Rosanna was, he said, "Look – I can't take you to the Channel Islands – it's too far, and a balloon acts far differently over water than it does over land. The best I can do is cross the Channel at its narrowest point and land in France. You will then have to make your way overland to St Malo where you can catch a ferry to any of the islands."

Rosanna thought about it and quickly realized they would never get a better offer to continue their escape and she smile and nodded her consent.

"I need to make some calculations concerning the weight that I will be carrying and the flight path we will take." Andrew looked about him then examined the sky. "Weather conditions are favourable at present and the forecast is promising for the next two days. If everything is OK, we can leave tomorrow."

The children offered to help Andrew to unload the equipment from the trailer and Rosanna went to inform Joseph of the latest developments. When everything was unloaded and spread out in an orderly fashion, Andrew began to assemble the balloon. Chris and Mirela watched in fascination as the envelope (the actual fabric balloon which holds the air) was unfolded and spread out over a large area. The skirt was propped open and the burner was then attached to the basket, then the basket canted at an angle so that when the burner was ignited, the hot air would flow into the envelope.

"Everything has to be checked thoroughly for safety's sake," explained Andrew. "So today I intend to inflate the envelope, tether the balloon and test that everything is working properly, making sure that the envelope has no tears in it."

"How high can you go in an air balloon, Mr Chambers?" asked Chris, bursting with curiosity.

"You can call me Andy, everyone else does. Sightseeing trips in a balloon usually keep to about five hundred to a thousand feet, but they can climb to ten thousand feet when necessary. What we need to do is to find our way to the Dover area where we can find a place to land, stay there overnight, and hopefully be blessed with fair winds and a continuing south-westerly breeze the next day that will take us across the Channel to France."

"You say the balloon acts differently travelling over water. Will we be safe flying over the Channel?" questioned Mirela, a little anxiously.

"Yes, quite safe," Andy reassured her. "Once we rise above the colder, shallow sea breeze, and the wind is blowing in the right direction, the flight should be quite uneventful."

The roar of the burners, when they were ignited, curbed any more attempts at conversation, so the children watched spellbound as the balloon gradually inflated to its enormous size and rose a few feet from the ground to be held there by its tethers. Andy fussed about doing adjustments here and there and when satisfied, they returned to the farmhouse leaving the balloon hovering in its place, ready for the next day.

Just as they were about finished with their evening meal, the telephone shrilled and Joseph answered it. He came back into the dining room several minutes later looking grim.

"Bad news I'm afraid," he said, when Rosanna looked at him enquiringly. "That was a call from a friend of mine who works in the Tourist Information Office in Ilfracombe. It seems someone has been making enquiries as to where they could find my farm, and they asked for me by name." Joseph pursed his lips in puzzlement. "She didn't like the look of them, so she told them that she didn't know because my name wasn't entered in the tourist accommodation ledger."

"How are they doing it?" Rosanna breathed with despair. "They always seem to be just a step behind us. It's only a matter of time before they arrive here. Where can we go Joseph? Where can we hide?"

Joseph paced up and down stroking his chin, and then stopping suddenly he said, "Quickly, gather up all your belongings, leave nothing behind and follow me."

Minutes later they followed Joseph, burdened by all their belongings and somewhat breathless, out to his truck and were bundled into the cab after piling everything in the rear cargo area. Joseph drove out of the gate and along the lane until they came to a track that led into a small wood. Driving into the wood, they stopped in a spot completely surrounded by trees and they watched as Joseph strode into a small clearing, reached into a hole in the trunk of a nearby tree, and an opening appeared in the ground, which revealed a set of steps that descended into darkness. Joseph descended the steps and disappeared from sight to reappear a few moments later and gestured for Rosanna and the children to follow him. Consumed by curiosity and a little hesitant, the children followed Rosanna and Joseph down the steps and into a spacious underground chamber that was lit by several oil lamps, providing enough illumination for them to look around and gawk at the clusters of arms, the stacks of tinned food and crude comforts that would sustain a person for many weeks.

"What is this place, Joseph?" asked Rosanna, looking around, mystified. "This looks to be more of a bunker than a place of shelter."

"Better bring your stuff down here and find a place for it, then I'll explain," instructed Joseph as he led the way back up the steps.

Later, when they had settled in and Joseph had closed the hatch, he began. "I've been sworn to secrecy never to reveal anything to anyone about this place but, needs must in this situation. It's a place where I was to hide should the Germans have invaded, and to have fought guerrilla raids against them for as long as I could." He paused, thoughtful for a moment with a far off look in his eyes. "There are many places like this throughout the land and there were many men, like me, who were willing to make the Germans pay for invading our shores." Again, he paused and drew a deep breath. "I must ask you not to reveal anything about this place when you leave because it is regarded as secret knowledge. Meanwhile, I must leave you and return to the farm. I will come again and give the signal when I think it is safe." As he turned to leave he said, "Please don't touch any of the weapons. Some of the them are loaded and I don't want any accidents." With that said and a meaningful look at Chris, he climbed the steps, shutting the hatch behind him and closing the silence in.

Chapter Thirteen

Bruno Fletcher stared moodily out of the car window while he waited for Anton to return. They were parked in the main street of Braunton, a village about ten miles inland from Ilfracombe, while enquiries were made about Joseph Dudley's farm. They had wasted a lot of time trying to locate the farm. The country folk had been less than helpful in giving specific directions and when they did, it was with a confusing amount of gestures and hand waving. The car door opened, and Anton swung into the driving seat.

"At last, we seem to have reliable information. The farm is about three miles further on, heading east towards Barnstable. Soon be there," he grinned, as he pulled out from the kerb and gunning the engine raced out of the village leaving a cloud of exhaust fumes in their wake.

They stopped the car a short distance past the farm while Bruno studied a map of the area. He had been surprised when he saw the hot air balloon tethered behind the farmhouse. He had wondered why his quarry had fled this far into the West Country, thinking that they were intending to head for one of the small seaports scattered around the coast to escape in one of the many fishing boats that were for hire. But now he was certain that they were going to use the balloon to escape to somewhere he could only guess at, and where he would not be able to follow.

"What do you think, Boss?" asked Anton. "Do we storm the place and take the kid, and if he's not there, beat this Dudley character until he tells us where he's hiding?"

Bruno was silent for a while. He was not absolutely sure that this was the place where the grandmother and the children had taken refuge. Best to stake out the place and if they were here, they would show themselves sooner or later, then they could swoop and take them all.

"We will put a watch on the place. Give Gino the walkie-talkie, Anton, and check the radio receiver is working properly." Then turning to Gino he said, "There's a small hill to the right of the farm. I want you to establish yourself there and keep watch. If you see two children led by an old lady tell us immediately, then get down there as fast as you can and hold them until we arrive. Call in every thirty minutes. I mean to get them this time, they have been able to slip away from us far too often."

Bruno and Anton watched Gino make his way along the lane towards the small hill that Bruno had indicated. Marcel had survived the gunshot wound he had sustained whilst undercover as Michel, but it would be a while before he would join Bruno and his team again. Meanwhile, Anton had recommended that Gino take Marcel's place. It remained to be seen how well he could carry out his instructions.

***

Joseph settled by the window with a pair of binoculars in an upstairs bedroom. It was time to put the training he had once taken to good use. He had acquired skills in the use of small arms, unarmed combat, surveillance and many other counter measures that he would have used against the German invaders. He raised the binoculars to his eyes and swept the countryside, paying particular attention to a knoll a short distance away that was the highest point in the area. *That is where I would be if I was watching the farm,* he thought to himself. He had spoken with Andy and had asked him to keep a look out on the other side of the farm for anyone acting suspiciously. He had also asked him to ready the balloon for a dawn departure, and that if there were to be any interference to the plan then he, Joseph, would take care of it.

The lighting in the underground bunker was about adequate, but it left pools of dark shadow in each corner and filtered fitfully amongst the racks that held the cache of arms and ammunition. They had all slept fitfully and uncomfortably for several hours and Rosanna now hovered over a small spirit stove making a pot of tea, while Mirela sat close to a lamp reading one of the many books she had found stacked on a nearby shelf.

Chris prowled amongst the racks, looking at the large array of rifles and pistols. There was enough armament to supply several squads of soldiers. Chris was fascinated by the thought that the bunker would have been used in a secret way to take the war to the enemy. The temptation to pick up one of the pistols to examine it was overwhelming. He had had some instruction on how a pistol worked from a security guard when visiting a laboratory where his father had worked. Not being allowed into the restricted area, he had spent time at the gatehouse where a friendly guard had showed him how to use the safety catch, aim the pistol and to pull the trigger, with an empty gun, of course. He wandered back to where Rosanna sat drinking her tea. Taking the cup of hot sweet tea that Rosanna offered him, he sipped it in silence, until a few moments later, Mirela put down her book and came to join them.

"You're very quiet, Mirela," said Rosanna with concern, handing her a cup of tea. "Is there something bothering you?"

"I'm not sure, grandma," she answered, with a slight frown. "I have this feeling about the balloon, that all will not be well if we escape in it. But it could just be that I'm not looking forward to the flight because I don't like heights, and it really does seem to be a strange and risky way to travel."

Rosanna too had his vague feeling of unease about travelling in the balloon. It had begun several hours before when she had studied the hugely inflated envelope and the ridiculously small basket in which they were to travel, dangling beneath it. Mirela's heightened sense of foreboding had seldom been wrong, but what alternative did they have if they were to escape the clutches of those who hunted them.

"Oh! Come on Mirela," enthused Chris. "It will be fun. We will soar into the sky on silent wings and we will be able to see for miles and miles."

Mirela smiled faintly. She didn't want to alarm Chris too much, but the ominous feeling of danger was growing stronger with each hour. She would have to contain it as best she could.

The series of knocks that was the signal they had agreed upon with Joseph came, halting any further conversation. The trapdoor swung open and Joseph descended the steps.

"Hurry, we must go now, collect your things. It will be dawn in thirty minutes. Andy is ready to fire up the burners, you must be away before the warning is passed on to those hunting you."

Joseph strode to the racks and selected a rifle, a handgun and a box of ammunition, then led the way out into the darkness. Chris lagged behind and on his way past the racks, he snatched a pistol off the same shelf and stuffed it in his holdall. It was still dark, but as they left the wood there was a light streak in the eastern sky that heralded the coming of dawn.

Arriving at the balloon, breathless after their hurried exit from the wood, Andy was there to greet them.

"I'm afraid we have lost the south-easterly and now have a southerly condition," he said, ruefully. "I cannot take you to Dover, but we will leave here and hopefully find a place that will be safe for you. I can only allow one small bag each, I must keep the weight down as much as possible," he added. "I will be firing the burners in the next few minutes to inflate the envelope to full capacity. Be ready to take your places in the basket when I signal you, then we can get under way."

When the burners were ignited there was the expected roar that Joseph knew would warn the watcher on the nearby knoll that the balloon was planning to leave. He moved away from the balloon into the shadows with his rifle, ready should anyone appear. It seemed an interminable time before Andy signalled for his passengers to climb aboard.

Feeling a rush of relief, Joseph stepped forward intending to release the tethers that would allow the balloon to lift into the dawn sky, when a gun was thrust painfully into the small of his back and a harsh voice ordered him to drop his rifle and raise his hands. Joseph, taken completely by surprise, complied immediately and was pushed, stumbling forward, toward the balloon. Surprise and consternation showed on the faces of Rosanna and the children when they saw what was happening. Andy, a guarded look on his face, dropped his hand from the lever, silencing the roar of the burners abruptly and allowing the quietness to rush in and capture the tableau in all its stillness. The man moved from behind Joseph, keeping his gun trained on his captive and called to Andy.

"Stay where you are, all of you, and keep your hands away from that lever. None of you are going anywhere."

Joseph looked at his captor, trying to gauge the man's abilities and his strength of purpose. Perhaps he had some military training for he had been very quick arriving after the burners set up their confounded roar. He was of average height and slim with a hard look to his face. He wore a cap, pulled low, the peak hiding much of his eyes and he spoke with a rough continental accent.

"Whom do you work for? What do you want with Rosanna and the children?" asked Joseph, dropping his hands and moving a step closer. The man stood his ground and lifted the gun pointing it at Joseph's head.

"Stay where you are and keep your mouth shut, or I will shoot you without hesitation," snarled the man.

Chris ducked down in to the basket while the gunman's attention was centred on Joseph, dipped into his holdall and pulled out the pistol. He grunted with satisfaction when he saw that it was indeed loaded, pushed the safety catch off and standing up levelled the pistol at the gunman and pulled the trigger.

The unexpectedly loud explosion and the strong kick of the weapon caused Chris to stagger back, hitting the basket wall behind him. He saw the gunman's figure jerk and stagger back several paces, a surprised look on his face, his gun arm dropping as though his handgun had become too heavy to hold. In an instant Joseph was upon him, grasping the wrist that held the gun and delivering a chopping blow with the edge of his hand to the gunman's neck. The man collapsed, and Joseph scooped up the gun, released the hammer, and stuck it in his belt. The sound of a car engine coming fast hastened Joseph to the balloon to start releasing the tethering ropes. Andrew immediately ignited the burners causing the balloon to pull at the mooring ropes as though impatient to become airborne. Undoing the last tether, Joseph called to Rosanna.

"I will find out where you are, and I will come to you. Take care and good luck." He gave Chris a severe look and with a slight edge to his voice he said, "I think I know where you got the pistol from young man. We will discuss it next time we meet. Give it to Rosanna for safekeeping. Goodbye."

As soon as the last tether was released the balloon rose gracefully in to the dawn sky gaining height rapidly. Joseph waved goodbye then ran to the barn, picking up his rifle on the way. He climbed into the hayloft and prepared to give the occupants in the car a warm welcome.

The car swerved in through the gate and raced up the road towards the farmhouse, but suddenly screeched to a halt when the driver caught sight of the balloon sailing overhead. Anton, the tall blonde man, leapt out of the car and opening the boot, he took out a rifle with a telescopic sight and began firing rapidly, emptying the magazine at the bulk of the envelope in the hope of inflicting enough damage to make the balloon lose height. He soon had to duck back into the car when a bullet hit the car roof and spun off close to his head. His priority now was to follow the balloon, hoping for an opportunity to put another fusillade of bullets into the fabric before it gained the height that would put it out of range. Ramming the car into reverse, he careered back down the road toward the gate, chased by shots from the hidden gunman firing from the vicinity of the barn.

They turned and twisted though the lanes keeping the balloon in sight, but the distance was always too great for them to take any more pot shots at it. They decided they would follow it to get the general direction in which it was going, and perhaps by studying the map, they might get an idea of where it would land.

Bruno was fuming. When he had taken the call from Gino he was sure that the boy would soon be in his hands, but Gino had not been able to hold on to them. Somehow, they had been able to neutralize him. It made him think that perhaps they had some way of knowing he was closing in, or they had luck on their side. Now he would have to send for more men and that did not come cheap. Then Anton's shout broke into his thoughts.

"It looks like they are lower in the sky. Perhaps they have sustained some damage."

Bruno watched the balloon for several minutes. It did seem to be lower. At this stage it should have been gaining height to stay out of range of the firing.

"Stay on its trail, Anton. Keep it in sight. We mustn't lose it. This damn chase is taking far too long and the people becoming involved are not the kind I want snooping around." Then, with exasperation he said, "Do you know that my informants warned me that farmer Joseph used to be with MI5? That is not good. We can do without the complication of arousing the interest of Government Agencies. The sooner we have that boy in the bag, the sooner we can leave the country."

Chapter Fourteen

Andy glanced anxiously up inside the balloon to reaffirm the parachute valve was closed. This valve was used to allow the hot air to escape, to lose height, or to land. He had been firing the burners every few minutes to gain height, to take them out of rifle range, but so far, they had stayed at the same height, which was troubling. One of the bullets fired at them had ricocheted off the burner casing, perhaps it had gone on to cause damage elsewhere.

He glanced at his passengers to see if they had noticed anything. Mirela had been studying Andy closely and had a suspicion that all was not well, but her immediate concern was Chris. He was slumped on the floor of the basket, his face set and a look of despair in his eyes. She went and sat next to him, put her arm through his and looked into his eyes.

"I didn't mean to kill him, Mirela," Chris cried, brokenly. "I just pointed the gun at him and somehow it went off. I just wanted him to drop his gun."

"What are you saying child?" Rosanna asked from her position opposite them. "You didn't kill anyone. Mirela and I saw the gunman attempting to get to his feet when we were rising in the balloon, and Joseph binding the man's hands."

Chris's eyes widened and he blinked rapidly. "But I saw the man fall when I fired, and he lay still. Perhaps he was wounded badly enough to die later, so I will still be the one who killed him."

"We don't know where the bullet struck, but it won't help to blame yourself, Chris," said Mirela. "We will only find out if the man survived when, and if, we meet up with Joseph again. So, let's not dwell on it. Let's just be grateful we were able to escape, however it came about."

But their discussion was to be short-lived. The balloon was sinking lower in the sky and it seemed inevitable that they would land sooner than later.

"I can't maintain any height. The rifle fire must have done some damage, a tear somewhere in the envelope," explained Andy. "Air is escaping from the balloon. All we can hope is that the burners can replace enough air for us to have a soft landing, but if the tear worsens we will have to prepare for a crash landing, so cross your fingers and hold on to the basket straps for all you are worth."

The balloon slowly sank lower as they glided over the countryside with the accompanying roar of the burners loud in their ears. Andy stared up into the bowels of the balloon, praying that the envelope would remain intact long enough for them to land. Glancing down, he estimated that they still had about two hundred feet to go. The only obstructions below were the hedges bordering the fields. There was a stiff breeze blowing, if they could avoid the hedges they may land quite safely. Time seemed to pass slowly as they descended towards a fallow pasture, and Andy was preparing to shut down the burners when at fifty feet the envelope suddenly began to collapse, and the balloon dropped like a stone.

"Hold on for your life," Andy yelled, as he completed shutting down the burners and tucked himself into a corner of the basket. The basket smashed into the earth and bounced onto its side. The burner housing, connected to the basket, broke away and the basket, dragged by the partly inflated envelope, crashed into a nearby hedge and came to rest amongst uprooted hawthorn bushes and broken branches.

There was silence, and nothing moved for several minutes. Chris, shaken, but otherwise unhurt, fought to extricate himself from the tangle of branches and undergrowth that now filled the basket. Next to him Mirela, dazed and half-stunned, was trying ineffectively to push her way through the obstruction. Chris could see Rosanna slumped nearby, not moving, and the groans he heard seemed to be coming from Andy.

"Here, let me help you Mirela, we'll soon have you out of there," he said encouragingly, clearing away some of the debris that would allow her to crawl out of the basket and into the field. He made her lay down to give her time to recover, then went to see what he could do for Andy and Rosanna.

Andy had been injured in the impact when the burner housing had come loose and fallen across his right leg. Then he and the housing had been thrown out when the basket had bounced across the field. Chris made him as comfortable as he could, but he could see that Andy's leg was twisted and at an unnatural angle and he was in severe pain. Crawling back into the basket, Chris cleared a way, so he could reach Rosanna.

She had recovered consciousness and as he took her hand and leaned over her she smiled faintly. He moved to put an arm under her to lift her, but she held up her hand to stop him.

"What is it Rosanna? What are you trying to tell me?" he asked.

Rosanna smiled again and raise her hand to caress Chris's face. "I think there is something very wrong with my back and it would not be good to move me."

She caught her breath and winced as she moved slightly to ease her position.

"How is Mirela? Is she injured? Tell me, quickly."

"She was slightly stunned, but she will be alright," Chris reassured her.

"Then you must go, both of you, leave here quickly before the hunters arrive. They will have seen the balloon come down and they will be here soon." He was about to protest, but again she held up her hand to silence him. "People will have seen us come down, so emergency services will be on their way. Have Mirela come and say goodbye to me, quickly."

Chris went to see Andy, while Mirela was with her grandmother.

"I understand why you must go, Chris," said Andy, in a voice made hoarse with pain. "Make your way to Clovelly. Ask for a fisherman named Arthur Trevilian. Give him my name. Tell him that I wish him fair winds and full nets, he will help you."

Mirela emerged from where her grandmother lay, looking dejected and tearful. Chris took her hand and with a brief, regretful look back, they fled across the fields, stopping only at a nearby cottage to make sure that the occupants had informed the emergency services of the crash and to ask the quickest way to Clovelly.

They had been informed that it was about ten miles to Clovelly. They passed through the small villages of Almiston Cross and Cranford, stopping only when it was necessary for Mirela to rest, which indicated that she had not recovered fully from the blow to her head that she had sustained in the crash.

Arriving above the village, tired from their hurried journey, they sat to rest. Mirela, looking pale and worn, rested her head against a wall and allowed the sun's warm rays to caress her face. Her eyes drooped, and she was soon asleep. Chris too was enjoying the brief respite, but he had caught sight of figures below labouring up the steep, cobbled street towards them. As they came closer, he saw it was a man leading three donkeys laden with baskets. Chris stood and approached the man as he came abreast of them.

"Excuse me, sir. Can you tell me where we can find an Arthur Trevilian? I believe he is a fisherman and he lives in this village."

The man, short and rotund, wearing a cloth cap and rough working clothes, paused and smiled at Chris. It was nice to meet a polite youngster. It had been a long time since he had been called "Sir."

"Aye! Arthur Trevilian does indeed live here, but he is out in his boat and won't be docking for some hours yet. I will be returning down the hill shortly, so I can show you where he lives. His wife will be at home, so you can speak to her."

Chris thanked the man and watched as he led the donkeys onto a small plateau and unloaded the baskets that seemed to contain ashes from the village home fires. When the man returned he looked at Chris searchingly, taking in his dishevelled appearance, the scratches on his face, legs and arms and Mirela's similar appearance, but his concern was increased by the paleness of her face and the look of exhaustion.

"Who are you with?" he asked, looking around.

"It's complicated," said Chris. "That's why we need to find Mr Trevilian."

"Right-ho," said the man. "Wake your friend and she can ride Sparky. She doesn't look as if she could make it down the hill on her own."

Chris nudged Mirela awake, and the man lifted her on to his lead donkey, then they started their return journey down along towards the breakwater in the distance. Mirela, although she felt weak and her head ached continuously, was still able to appreciate the character and the charm of the village as she swayed gently to the donkey's gait. The white cottages on either side of the narrow lane and the alleyways that branched off at angles produced splashes of pleasantly-scented flowers of mixed colours that hung in baskets and overflowed from window boxes along the way. Here and there a tub or pot, placed randomly, supplemented the scene with a fusion of wild flowers that attracted bees in large numbers and added a background hum that contributed to the peacefulness of the day. Mirela, totally enchanted with Clovelly, could not cease to wonder how the houses clung to the impossibly steep side of the hill without toppling into the sea.

The man was describing his daily duties to Chris and pointing out visible outstanding features of the village.

"There is no other mode of transport other than the donkeys. No bicycles, no carts, and of course, no cars. Villages use sledges to move stuff down the hill, but to bring stuff up we use the donkeys. Ashes, rubbish, parcels, equipment and fish landed from the boats. Teams of donkeys are such an essential part of village life, they bring everything up."

They halted about two thirds of the way down the hill and the man lifted Mirela from Sparky. He directed them along an alley where he said they would find a number of stored lobster pots next to a cottage. This, he said, was where they would find the home of Arthur Trevilian. They thanked the man for his help, and after patting Sparky, they parted and made their way to the cottage that they had been directed to. The door was flung opened to their knock and a small, prim, middle-aged woman stood there. She wore a high-collared, gingham dress that almost swept the floor and a severe look on her face. Her mouth was opened as though to say something, but the words were never uttered. A slightly perplexed frown registered on her face as she regarded them, then she stepped out of the door to look up and down the alleyway, looking to see where the adults were.

"Can you tell me if this is the home of Mr Trevilian, Mr Arthur Trevilian?" asked Chris, in a small voice.

"Yes, this is where he lives," answered the woman, her frown deepening. "I am his wife. Perhaps you can explain to me why you wish to see him?"

Chris looked sideways at Mirela and shuffled his feet, not comfortable under the questioning gaze of the woman.

"Please forgive the unexpected visit Mrs Trevilian," said Mirela, apologetically. "But it is urgent that we speak with your husband as soon as possible. We were told to come here for help by Andy Chambers, the balloonist, after we were involved in an accident in which he was injured."

The frown cleared slightly at this news and Mrs Trevilian examined the two children a little more closely. By their worn look they seemed to have been through a rough experience. They looked tired and hungry, but it was the girl's pale, wan appearance that concerned her most. Making a swift decision she ushered them into the house.

The warm, inviting smell of baking made the children realize how long it had been since they had last eaten, and they looked hungrily at the cakes and pasties cooling on the kitchen table.

Noticing this, Mrs Trevilian said authoritatively, "You both need to clean yourselves up before you sit at the table. I have some warm water ready. Later, I will repair your torn cloths and try to make you look a little more presentable."

Later, after they had eaten their fill, Mrs Trevilian packed the children off to bed for they were obviously so tired that they could hardly keep their eyes open. When her husband arrived home, with fish for the evening meal, he was greeted with the news that he had two young visitors who had brought news of his friend Andy.

The fisherman and his wife looked at each other, their faces mirroring the perplexity they felt. What the children had informed them of was so far removed from their quiet, sedate way of life that they had difficulty grasping the full seriousness of the plight the two children were in. Arthur questioned the children closely, then after lighting his clay pipe and puffing furiously on it for several minutes, he ambled to the door in a swirl of tobacco smoke and went out to pace up and down past the window deep in thought.

Later, re-entering the house, Arthur sat in his fireside chair and asked the children several more questions. Then after more thought he made a decision.

"Firstly, we must find out if there are any suspicious strangers lurking around looking for you. Then, when it is dark, I will take you, Mirela, to see a retired doctor friend of mine who lives in the village. Although you have rested you still look peaky. The blow you received to your head may have given you a slight concussion and it will need to be treated." Arthur paused to repack his pipe with tobacco, then continued. "I will also take the opportunity to telephone Exeter Hospital, where I think Andrew and your grandmother will have been taken, assuming that their injuries are as serious as I think they are." Arthur looked askance at his wife. "Will you come with me Beatrice, while I deliver some fish? Your eyes are sharper than mine and you will notice more about any strangers wandering around, other than the normal tourists."

Later, when they returned to the cottage, both the Trevilians looked pensive. The fisherman glanced at his wife, who gave a slight nod of her head as they silently agreed what they must say.

"We noticed one man who seemed to be paying more than a little interest to those who entered the village, and to those who left," explained Arthur. "A rough looking individual who didn't seem to fit. There could possibly be more men stationed around the village, so we will have to be very careful when we move around."

It was agreed that Chris would stay with Mrs Trevilian while Mirela, dressed in a bonnet and long dress that was more in-keeping with village children's attire, accompanied Arthur through the darkened village on a circuitous path to the doctor's house.

When Mirela had taken the medication prescribed by the doctor and had been packed off to bed to sleep off her exhaustion, Chris, impatient to hear what news Arthur had of Andy and Rosanna, asked, "Were you able to get in touch with the hospital Mr Trevilian? Do you have any news of the casualties involved in the balloon crash?"

"Yes, I do, young man," he remarked tiredly. He had been up with the dawn to set his nets in Bideford Bay, as he did daily, and he was usually sound asleep at this late hour. But these were unusual times and he felt a paternal responsibility toward these two young and vulnerable children. He knew he and his wife would do their utmost to keep them from falling into the hands of those who would harm them. Blinking his eyes rapidly to ease the grittiness behind the lids, he stifled a yawn and continued. "Forgive my weariness Chris. I am no longer a young man and it is well past my bedtime. However, I was able to speak with Andy on the telephone and he informed me he is in good hands, but he will have to suffer his badly broken leg in traction for some time. As for Rosanna, she has a painfully strained back, severe bruising and a dislocated hip, which will also keep her in hospital for some weeks." Arthur paused and was silent for a moment. "Andy also described how lucky they were that the emergency services arrived when they did. It seems that the men who had been shooting at them were closing in but had to leave hurriedly when they heard the police arriving." Arthur stood and stretched. "And now young man I must go to my bed, or I won't be fit to do any fishing tomorrow."

"Goodnight, Mr Trevilian," said Chris. "Thank you for all the help you have given us, I really don't know what we would have done without you."

Arthur grunted and with a wave of his hand disappeared up the stairs to his room.

Chapter Fifteen

Mirela awoke the next morning, slowly becoming aware of where she was. Her headache had gone, and she felt much better. Glancing at the clock she calculated that she had slept for about fourteen hours and realized she was feeling very hungry. She tumbled out of bed and padded across the landing to Chris's room where she sat in a chair and watched him sleeping. Again, she was reminded of how much he looked like an angel, with his tousled blonde hair and his innocent face relaxed in the deep repose of slumber. She called him several times before he opened his eyes and stared balefully at her.

"What time is it?" he asked.

"It's breakfast time, and I'm starving. Come on, get up. I can smell what we're going to have and I'm more than ready for it. I'll see you downstairs."

After breakfast, when she and Chris were doing the washing up and Mrs Trevilian was preparing the ingredients for a pie, Mirela asked, "Are you familiar with poetry, Mrs Trevilian?"

"Yes! I know some poetry. Why do you ask?"

Mirela hesitated, starting to wonder if she would be believed if she were to carry on.

"I had a strange dream last night. I dreamt of a boat capsizing in a terrible storm and sinking with all its crew. Then I saw a man in strange clothes, sitting at a desk writing a poem. The poem was 'The Three Fishers'. Do you know of it?"

Mrs Trevilian stopped what she was doing and stared at Mirela, a slightly puzzled look on her face.

"Yes! I know of it. Charles Kingsley, a well-known Victorian author, wrote it. He actually lived here in this cottage as a young man. Are you sure you didn't learn it in school?"

"No! But I know it now, would you like me to recite it?"

"I'm sorry Mirela, perhaps later, I have a meeting at The Women's Institute. You know you must remain in the house of course – I won't be gone too long."

Mirela sat deep in thought while Chris tidied up and placed the remaining clean dishes in a cupboard, then came and sat beside her. He looked at her questioningly, a slight frown furrowing his brow.

"Have you had many of that type of dream before, Mirela?" he asked.

"No! Only the occasional flashback that I wasn't able to make much sense of," she admitted. "I seem to have absorbed a scene from the past out of the very fabric of the cottage. It's extraordinary how vivid everything was," she paused as she reflected on the likelihood of it happening again.

"Now that you are able to see things from the past, perhaps you will also be able to see things from the future," pondered Chris. "Your grandmother did say that your psychic abilities would continue to increase with time. It could be that this is what is happening now."

"Yes! Perhaps so," agreed Mirela. "I do wish she were here now, so she could explain things to me and reassure me in her gentle, sensible way. It would help me to adjust easier to whatever other gifts I am to possess."

The hours seemed to pass interminably slow, until Mrs Trevilian returned followed shortly afterwards by her husband. After the evening meal when they were all gathered around the fire, and Mr Trevilian was puffing on his pipe, he began to tell of the day's happenings.

"After the day's fishing, I called into Bideford harbour where I hoped to see a friend of mine, the skipper of a schooner, *The Dolphin*, that trades around the channel ports of England and France. I asked him if he could carry two young passengers to the Channel Isles, giving a brief explanation that your parents wanted you to join them. But they were preparing to set sail on the tide to ports along the Cornish coast, calling at the Scilly Isles, then continuing to the Channel Isles and France." Arthur paused and leaning over knocked his pipe on the hearth to dislodge the ash that had built up, then he continued. "I managed to persuade him to take you on board when he arrives in the Scilly Isles, so we must make preparations for you to leave here, hopefully, undetected." Arthur leaned back in his seat glancing at his wife who returned his look and nodded.

"We – the members of The Women's Institute – had a meeting today to discuss how best we could disrupt the attention of the men we suspected of being here to watch for signs of you two children." Beatrice paused and smiled knowing that she had the children's full attention. "Members will be watching for anyone who does not fit in, and for persons who are seeming to be too observant. The women will report to me, so we will know their descriptions, and then we can build up a picture of their activities." Beatrice paused and turning to her husband asked, "How soon will you want to sail for the Isles of Scilly, Arthur?"

"In three days' time, *The Dolphin* should arrive at the Scilly Isles on the fourth day at the latest." Arthur looked quizzically at Mirela and said, "Now that we have discussed our plans, perhaps you can tell us of this strange dream that you had when you dreamt about Charles Kingsley and his poetry."

Mirela began a little shyly, but when she saw how much interest the Trevilians displayed she felt more confident. She described the dream and then recited the poem. "Three fishers went sailing..."

Time dragged slowly by for Chris and Mirela. They were impatient to leave the confines of the cottage and do more than just keep out of sight. Although the Trevilians had given them several games to play with, there was a limit to the amount of interest they provided. Especially when they began to argue as to who was cheating the most.

On the morning of the day before they were to leave, Mrs Trevilian announced that there was to be a special event to take place.

"We need to get you on board the fishing boat this evening, so Arthur can start the journey to the Scilly Isles in the early hours of tomorrow morning. I have arranged with the committee of The Women's Institute to have all the children of the village gathered at the village fountain for an out-of-season practise of Lentsherd, or better known as Tin Can Night." Mrs Trevilian held up her hand to forestall the questions that Chris and Mirela were bursting to ask. "We need to create a diversion whereby you will not be noticed among the many other children who will be there. We will disguise you, and you will both take part in the event which will start at the top of the village and end at the quay, where it should be easy for you to slip aboard the boat."

"What is Lentsherd?" asked Mirela, speaking up first. "And what will we have to do to take part?"

"Lentsherd is a custom that has been passed down for hundreds of years. It is an event that happens each Shrove Tuesday where children tie tin cans to themselves and drag them along the cobbles to the quay to frighten away the evil spirits and drive the Devil into the sea, before the Holy Season of Lent begins the following day."

"That sounds like fun," grinned Chris. "Will there be many other children there?"

"Enough of them to make quite a din, I should think," smiled

Mrs Trevilian, then her face became serious. "There is one important precaution we must take. If for any reason you can't get on board the fishing boat, I will be there to take you to Crazy Kate's Cottage, which is right on the quay. There we will wait until it is safe to do so."

"Who is Crazy Kate?" Chris and Mirela asked in unison, their eyes wide with curiosity. "Was she really crazy?"

"It's a sad story about a woman who became demented with grief," began Mrs Trevilian. "Kate Lyall died in 1736. Her house looks out over the harbour and she used to watch her husband from an upper window as he fished in the bay. One day a squall blew up just outside the harbour. Kate watched as the boat capsized and her husband drowned. From that time on, she began acting very strangely. One day she put on her wedding dress and walked into the sea to join her husband in his watery grave."

"Oh! That poor woman," exclaimed Mirela, her eyes reflecting the sadness she felt.

"Yes!" agreed Mrs Trevilian. "When people earn their living from the sea, it does take its toll. Now, we must organize ourselves for the event tonight."

Chapter Sixteen

There was quite a crowd gathered at the fountain that evening. The rattle of the tin cans was continuous as the children moved around testing and tugging the string tied to their waists. Chris and Mirela mingled among the crowd of excited children, woollen hats pulled low on their heads and clothing in-keeping with what was worn by the rest of the company. Suddenly, there was a shout for everyone to get ready, then a whistle shrilled for the run to begin.

There was some jostling as everyone shuffled forward, then they were off, pelting down the steep hill with the tin cans setting up a terrific din as they rattled and bounced around on the cobbles. People lined the way, clapping and cheering as the children went by. The older children at the front charged down the steep thoroughfare, each competing to be first to reach the quay. The younger ones bringing up the rear at a less frantic pace. There was the occasional trip which sent a youngster tumbling to the ground, to be lifted up, set back on their feet, dusted down and sent on their way again.

Chris and Mirela held hands as they ran so they could stay together in the middle of the group, their ears ringing with the noise of crashing and bouncing containers and the high-pitched voices of the children calling to each other. Mirela was revelling in the occasion. With her heightened awareness and the excitement of the occasion, the colours of the other children's' auras were a kaleidoscope of moving, bobbing, living colour, surrounding her on all sides. Normally, when she saw auras they were just faint outlines tracing peoples' upper bodies. But when she was stimulated by something, or concentrating on someone, the colours glowed brightly with varying degrees of intensity. Soon, they arrived at the quay where the children continued to run, but formed tight circles, often around several captured adults who held their hands over their ears to lessen the invasive noise.

Chris and Mirela saw Mrs Trevilian close to Crazy Kate's Cottage. She was staring intently towards the hotel and beckoned Chris and Mirela to her side. She spoke briefly to one of the women nearby who called to a group of children and then led them towards the hotel where a stall had been set up to serve drinks and snacks to the children. They gathered about a man and a woman and began to run in circles around them. A group of women also gathered laughing and talking as they watched the children, effectively hemming the couple in and diverting their attention.

"Quickly, we must go aboard the boat now while we have the opportunity," said Beatrice urgently.

Taking Chris and Mirela by the hand. they hurried past the hotel to the edge of the quay, and descending the steps, climbed aboard a boat to find Arthur Trevilian waiting for them. Arthur ushered them down below into a cabin where there was an oil lamp suspended above a table surrounded by bench seats and several bunks lining the walls. Beatrice produced some drinks and snacks for Chris and Mirela and they all sat at the table where Arthur explained that the two children must stay on board the boat until they were able to sail the next morning.

"We had identified the man and the woman who were on the quay as two who were watching for you," Beatrice explained. "They had asked the hotel staff if they had noticed any new children staying in the village recently. The staff told them nothing and their suspicions were passed on to us."

Mirela remained silent, while Chris enthused about the run through the village and down to the quay, saying what fun it had been.

"Are there any crew on board, Mr Trevilian?" asked Mirela, suddenly interrupting the conversation and glancing to the companionway that led onto the deck.

"No, I have two crew, but they will not arrive on board until we are due to sail. Why do you ask?"

"Oh! Just curious," she said uncertainly, her attention once again drifting towards the stairway.

Chris looked searchingly at Mirela. He had been around her long enough to know when she was troubled and that she sensed something was not quite right. Leaving the table, he made his way to the companionway, muttering that he wouldn't be long.

Reaching the deck, he glanced around. All was dark except for a fitful light that filtered down from the quay making the shadows seem even more intense, which presented a challenge to his ever-fertile imagination. He made his way carefully along the deck to an open hatch where equipment was kept, the ever-present smell of fish pervading his nostrils. He stood still, listening. All was quiet except for the sound of water lapping against the hull and the occasional unidentified creak or groan that all vessels seemed to make as part of their way of communicating with the crew. Turning to retrace his steps, he suddenly heard a whisper of movement from behind, but before he could whirl around, strong arms seized him, hoisted him off his feet and a hand was cupped over his mouth, smothering the shout of alarm before it could leave his lips. Chris struggled and attempted to bite down on the hand, but his jaw was grasped more firmly, and a voice whispered close to his ear.

"Hello Chris, I told you I would find you. You know who I am. I am going to release you now – you're not armed, are you?"

When his feet touched the deck, Chris turned and took a step back looking up at the tall figure before him.

"Joseph – what – how?"

"Let's join the others young man, then I can explain how I got here. You lead the way."

When Chris descended the companionway, followed by Joseph, the Trevilians reacted with a mixture of surprise and concern and were even more mystified when Mirela leapt to her feet and running to Joseph she flung herself into his arms. Joseph hugged her and chuckled.

"I told you I would find you. Now, introduce me to these good people who have been protecting you."

Having calmed their fears and reassured the Trevilians that he wasn't a threat, Joseph was able to tell them of the unrelenting hunt to kidnap the children and the desperate chase that had brought them to Clovelly.

"I'm sorry to barge in on you in this way, but I just couldn't go around asking questions, so I decided to find out which your boat was and stow away aboard it. I had no idea that you had planned the children's escape for tonight, so I was very fortunate to have decided to get on board when I did."

"Have you any news of my grandmother and Andy, Joseph?" asked Mirela anxiously.

"Yes, Mirela. When I heard of the crash landing I was so worried about you. I got in touch with the police and they were able to inform me that two injured people had been taken to Exeter Hospital. When I visited the hospital, I spoke with your grandmother and Andy who told me that you had fled to Clovelly, hoping to find and get help from Arthur Trevilian. Thankfully, you could not have found shelter in a better place, and I will be forever thankful to Arthur and Beatrice for their inventiveness and protection at such a time. Your Grandmother has a badly wrenched back, a dislocated hip and some serious bruising, but with treatment and rest she should recuperate in time. Trevor's badly broken leg is more serious, and he will have to have more surgery to repair the bone."

The Trevilians stood and made preparation to leave.

"I may as well go back to the cottage with Beatrice now that I know you will be here, Joseph. We will be sailing at five in the morning. There are adequate bunks for you all and you can find food in the galley – goodnight."

As the Trevilians footsteps faded from the deck above, Chris, who had been fidgeting for a while blurted out, "What – what happened to the man who – er, got hurt?"

Joseph sat back and regarded Chris solemnly. "He sustained a rather bad wound and it had to be staunched often on the way to the hospital. The doctor said he was in a serious condition but would survive if operated on as soon as possible. I informed the police so that they could interview him when he recovered."

A weight seemed to lift from Chris's shoulders and he smiled with relief but became uncomfortable when Joseph continued to stare at him unwaveringly.

"You know Chris, what you did was a very foolish and dangerous thing, you could so easily have shot me, then where would we be?"

"I'm sorry Joseph, but I wanted some way to protect Mirela and myself from being kidnapped. We had come so near to being taken that I needed some way to defend ourselves."

Joseph pondered for a while, thinking about what Chris had said. Then he came to a decision. "Alright, we will not speak of it again, but as soon as we get an opportunity I will instruct you both in how to handle a firearm. Even if you never fire a gun again, you will at least know how to hold one and will have learnt the safety precautions that you need to know."

Chapter Seventeen

Chris awoke from a deep sleep and gradually became aware that the boat was underway. The pitching and rolling had become more pronounced now that they had left the harbour and were sailing out into the bay. This was his first experience of sailing and he was undecided whether he would like it.

Mirela was already up and about helping Joseph prepare breakfast and seemed to be coping well with the seemingly unpredictable movement of the boat. Chris placed his feet on the deck and standing, he cautiously took a step towards the table, but unprepared for the forward pitch, and to the amusement of his companions, he lost his balance and ended up sprawled on the deck close to the companionway. Things didn't improve for Chris, he became very seasick during the two-hour voyage and was only too glad when they made landfall in the Scilly Isles. Chris staggered ashore at St Mary's Isle looking pale and shaken, thankful to be once again on dry land.

They had but a short time to spend looking around before *The Dolphin* arrived to take them the rest of their journey. They bade Arthur Trevilian a reluctant goodbye and promised to visit him and his wife Beatrice at Clovelly one day. Chris and Mirela, preparing to board *The Dolphin*, waited on the quay while Joseph finished some last-minute business. They examined the clean, graceful lines of the ship's hull and stared up at the masts that towered above them. Mirela linked her arm in Chris's, wanting to reassure him that everything would be alright.

"Perhaps with it being a bigger ship it will not pitch and roll as much as the fishing boat, so you may not be sick again."

"Perhaps not," Chris agreed, not totally convinced. He was apprehensive about the trip and dreaded the thought that he may be violently seasick again, but what choice did he have? Joseph arrived and stood behind them placing his hands on their shoulders.

"Isn't she just a wonderful sight. She is one of the last wooden-hulled three-masted schooners to still be plying her trade around the channel ports." He took in the length and breadth of *The Dolphin,* gazing at her with admiration. "Her length is 98.30 feet and her breadth is 23.15 feet, the depth of her hold is 10.16 feet which allows her to carry 250 tons of cargo. She was fitted with a 125 brake-horsepower diesel engine in 1943, so we will not be completely reliant upon the winds to make headway. Come along, it's time for us to get aboard, they will be casting off shortly."

They had but a short time to walk the deck before *The Dolphin* left the quay. Joseph pointed out the windlass and described its use when hoisting the sails and the rigging.

"There's an awful lot of rope used on board," Chris observed, as he tried to keep his mind off the queasiness he felt, even though the ship was rising and falling gently at her moorings.

"Actually, all the rigging on board has different names," explained Joseph. "There are halyards and shrouds and braces, but there is only one rope. I will let you discover what that rope is attached to. I will be generous and give you one clue," he smiled mysteriously. "It is used often, and used every day, even when the ship is berthed."

Soon, St Mary was dropping astern as *The Dolphin* ploughed strongly into a choppy sea before a freshening wind. Chris and Mirela had been quartered aft in the saloon, while Joseph took up residence in the forecastle. The skipper paid Chris a visit when he heard that he was once again being very sick.

"Not many people escape *mal de mer*, or seasickness, when they first venture to sea," stated the captain, looking down at Chris as he lay pale and listless in his bunk. "Here, eat this seed cake, but only with small sips of water. It will help to bind your stomach. I know you are very thirsty, but you must only take small sips of water to help you swallow the cake." Then with a smile he climbed the companionway to return to his duties on deck.

In contrast to Chris, Mirela revelled in being aboard *The Dolphin*. She stood, legs braced to the roll of the ship, her long hair streaming in the wind, listening to the sounds as it whistled and thrummed through the rigging. Occasionally, a mist of fine spray would be kicked up as the ship surged through the seas and Mirela would gasp as it showered her with its coldness. Like Chris, it was also her first introduction to the sea and although she was loving the experience, she was ever mindful of the vast, impersonal nature of the waters and the dangers which every vessel faced when putting to sea.

Later, when Mirela had returned to the cabin, she found Chris somewhat recovered and sleeping peacefully. She found a book to read and was immersed in the pages when Joseph paid a visit to inform them that there had been a weather warning of sudden squalls being whipped up between the islands, but there was no need to become alarmed as *The Dolphin* had weathered many a storm in her time. Mirela tried to return to her reading, but she found she could not concentrate. She had the feeling that all was not well since she had first stepped aboard *The Dolphin* but had put it down to her lack of experience on a seagoing vessel. She knew that she must not ignore the feeling but felt that there was not much she could do about the situation other than to be prepared for whatever may happen.

The two children were on deck as *The Dolphin* threaded its

way between the islands. They watched as Guernsey fell away to starboard and Mirela began to feel optimistic that they would reach Jersey without mishap within a few hours. Chris was feeling much better and was actually enjoying being on deck again.

Suddenly, a loud screeching noise was heard, accompanied by grinding and clanking, coming from below decks. A crewman nearby dropped what he was doing and sprinted to the companionway disappearing quickly down to the lower deck. The racket continued for several minutes, then all went quiet. The crewman appeared soon afterwards looking grim-faced and strode aft to report to the skipper. The skipper cursed when he was given the report and instructed the crewman to take the helm and strode aft. He could be seen leaning over the rail peering down into the depths. Mirela, curious as to what was going on, tugged Chris's sleeve, urging him to follow her. As they drew closer to the aft of the ship, the skipper stood back from the rail stroking his jaw in thought, then coming to a decision he stomped back to the wheel and could be heard telling the crewman that a hawser, probably jettisoned from another vessel, had caught in the propeller causing the engine to seize up.

"Damn those careless crews that discard hawsers overboard. It causes untold damage to smaller vessels," he shouted angrily. "Get the rest of the crew on deck and hoist more sail. We're going to be late arriving in Jersey."

The wind started to freshen, and *The Dolphin* ploughed through the seas in a lively way. The skipper, at the helm again, kept watch on the sails and the rigging as they filled and strained in the strengthening south-westerly. Occasionally, the skipper would glance at the horizon, calculating the strength of the wind and judging the state of the sea. At four bells the skipper was relieved by one of the crew and went below to plot their progress on the chart.

Chris and Mirela were in their cabin with Joseph when they heard the urgent call for the skipper to come on deck. The skipper appeared and quickly assessed the situation. The wind had increased in velocity and the sky had become dark with storm clouds. The sea was becoming increasingly rough and the ship was plunging and rolling in a more violent manner. The skipper shouted and gestured urgently to the crew.

"Get aloft and reduce as much sail as you can. There is a squall heading our way."

The skipper took over the helm and held the ship steady as much as he could. Joseph, now on deck with the children, made his way along the heaving deck to the skipper.

"Is there anything I can do, skipper?"

"This is going to be a bad, Joseph. If I had my engine we could run before the storm, but all we can do is to try to run before it and hope for the best." He continued to struggle to hold the helm as it bucked and jerked in his hands. "Take the children and yourself to the main mast. There you will find harnesses. Strap yourselves to the mast as securely as you can and pray that we survive this."

They made their way with difficulty across the heaving deck and Joseph explained what was happening to the frightened children as he secured them firmly into their harnesses.

"It is better that we secure ourselves here, in this way. If we stayed below and the ship was swamped, we could be trapped below deck unable to escape. This way there is more of a chance to leave the ship if we have to."

Mirela, her eyes wide with fear, looked around her at the now raging sea. The ship was behaving like a wild thing as it lurched and plunged in and out of the troughs. The wind shrieked with fury through the rigging while the crew desperately held on aloft as they tried to reduce as much canvas as possible. The skipper, with one of the crew, clung to the wheel trying to maintain the set course, if it hadn't been secured the helm would have been impossible to control. Everyone was soon drenched to the skin as spray was flung high overhead and the deck became awash with foaming seas.

Chris, his fear greater than anything he had ever known, prayed fervently for survival and promised himself that if he survived he would never set foot on another ship as long as he lived.

The storm seemed to have increased in intensity, when without warning, a hurricane-like gust of wind hit the ship broadside, tearing to shreds the remaining unfurled sails and making the ship heel over to port like a crippled animal. Shouts and screams ensued as the crew held on to prevent themselves be hurled into the sea. Joseph cursed aloud while Chris and Mirela screamed and sobbed with fright as they hung suspended in their harnesses over the seething seas. As the ship continued to heel over loud thuds could be heard as the cargo shifted below decks. It seemed an interminable time before the ship ceased to heel over. It lay floundering at a thirty-five-degree angle as the hungry sea washed over it, looking for any weakness that would allow it to take her plunging to the bottom. Joseph struggled to release his harness. He knew that there was very little time left before the ship completely capsized. All it would take would be another large wave and they would founder, and they would be lost. He struggled out of his harness and was working on Mirela's, when he heard the skipper's shouted command to abandon ship.

The crew began to try to launch the lifeboat, but it was almost impossible while the ship lay at such an acute angle. As the crew struggled with the launching procedure they suddenly became aware that the wind had dropped perceptibly. The skipper held up his hand for the crew to stop what they were doing, and everyone fell silent as they cautiously looked around and listened with bated breath as they sensed that the squall was past its worst. The skipper, with an expression of new hope on his face, turned to the crew, and with wonder in his voice he spoke.

"Abort that order to abandon ship, I do believe the old lady is trying to right herself." Almost imperceptibly the angle lessened as the ship struggled to become upright. "Quickly, into the hold all of you, we must help her to become upright by moving the cargo back into place."

The crew needed no more bidding, they hurled themselves into the hold and working like fiends they moved the jumble of cargo and stowed as much of it as they could in some kind of balanced order.

As they worked the skipper was gratified to see the ship gradually becoming more upright, until eventually, she stayed at a fifteen-degree list. The skipper felt an immense sense of relief and knew they had had a very narrow escape.

A radio mayday call had been made to the Jersey Lifeboat, which would hopefully arrive within the next hour or two to tow them into harbour. The pitifully small amount of canvas that remained was hoisted and the ship was able to make some headway, but progress was slow, and the ship often wallowed like a stricken whale. The pumps could be heard hammering away, spewing gallons of seawater out of the interior of the ship, which would hopefully lessen the list. Everything that could be done to keep the ship afloat had been done. The skipper, as he surveyed the damage that had been done to his beloved *Dolphin*, prayed fervently that there would not be another squall. He paced the listing deck, ever watchful of the horizon and mindful of the fresh wind that could blow up into a fury in no time.

It was quite dark, when almost two hours later, the lifeboat pulled alongside *The Dolphin*. A towing hawser was passed to *The Dolphin* and several more lines were passed between the vessels to rig up a bosun's chair, so that the passengers could be transferred to the lifeboat. When all was ready, Mirela was urged to go first. She climbed up and was strapped into the chair, then the lifeboat crew hauled on the line and with a gasp she was dangling precariously over the seas that heaved only feet below her. Mirela clung on desperately as the chair swung and bobbed its way slowly towards the deck of the lifeboat. The Coxswain unstrapped her from the chair and congratulated her on how brave she had been, then muffling her in a warm blanket he carried her below where she was given a delicious steaming mug of soup to await the transfer of the others. Chris arrived next, pale-faced, but grinning with bravado, then it was the turn of Joseph. With him being much heavier the chair had sagged alarmingly and had actually dipped into the sea, but arriving safely aboard the lifeboat he had the lifeboat crew grinning when he quipped.

"Can we do that again without me getting wet?"

The progress of both the vessels during the night was very slow, but eventually they entered the harbour at St Helier. It took painstaking manoeuvring to get *The Dolphin* berthed next to the quay, but when it was done, Joseph and the children gave their thanks to the lifeboat crew and proceeded to make their way ashore.

The sun was up when Joseph and the children climbed the ladder up to the quay. Chris felt a great sense of relief to be back on dry land again. The Harbour Master was waiting to greet them and as he approached, there was a sudden commotion from a building nearby and a group of people surged towards them clutching cameras and waving notebooks. The Harbour Master was pushed unceremoniously aside and Joseph, Chris and Mirela found themselves surrounded by a crowd of noisy, gesturing reporters. Camera bulbs flashed, and voices called questioningly in a most bewildering way.

"Can you tell us what it was like out there?" a voice bawled.

"Were you in any danger of capsizing when you were hit by the storm?" called another.

Joseph held the children close, shielding them, trying to hide their faces from the cameras. They were pushed and jostled as the mob competed with each other to get the first statement. This situation had not been expected and was the worst thing that could have happened. They were completely hemmed in and there seemed no escape.

"Please, try to have some thought for the children. Can't you see that they are distressed by all this," cried Joseph. "Why don't you go and interview the crew of *The Dolphin*. They will be able to tell you more than we can." But the plea fell on deaf ears and there was a fresh outburst of people calling for information.

Joseph looked desperately around for a way of escape, but just as he was about to try to force a way out, a shout went up as the Harbour Master led a group of customs men into the melee and reaching Joseph and the children, they were escorted to a group of offices nearby.

"Best if you stay here until we disperse the news hounds," said the Harbour Master. "I need to talk to the skipper of *The Dolphin* to find out what he plans to do about his ship and get him to fill in some paperwork. Is there anything else I can do for you?"

"I would like to make a telephone call to a friend to come and pick us up," said Joseph. "Thank you for rescuing us from that devilish situation. We were really not prepared for it."

"Not at all. Welcome to Jersey," smiled the Harbour Master, then hurrying away he joined with the customs men and headed towards *The Dolphin*.

***

Soon they were motoring along the front towards St Aubin, a charming, picturesque village a short distance from St Helier. They climbed winding roads until they reached a spacious bungalow overlooking St Aubin Bay. Chris and Mirela found the view breath-taking, for it took in the whole of St Aubin Bay with Elizabeth Castle and St Helier visible in the far distance. A housekeeper appeared soon after they arrived and busied herself making a welcome meal for the tired and hungry trio. After the meal, Joseph disappeared saying that he had some important arrangements to make, so Chris and Mirela, with their hunger satisfied, caught up on some much-needed sleep.

Joseph returned some hours later with the news that they would have to leave. "I'm sorry, but we will have to move again. It is essential that we find somewhere safer, somewhere where we will be less exposed," he explained. "I should have been prepared for the reporters at the dock and taken precautions against being found by the news media. The news of our survival and our arrival here will no doubt appear in the newspapers on the mainland, so the people hunting us will know where we have escaped to." He rubbed his eyes to dispel some of the tiredness he felt and then continued. "I contacted a colleague who lives on the island, and he has pulled some strings to allow us to stay at Corbiere Lighthouse. We can't enter the lighthouse until the tide ebbs this evening, then we will be able to reach the lighthouse across the causeway."

Chapter Eighteen

There had been no indication, nor any news, of the where the children were. They had simply vanished into thin air. Even his telephone link with the people whom he had relied on in the past to supply him with information, were unable to trace the two children. Bruno paced his hotel room raging with impatience. Time was of the essence. His paymasters had warned him that if they didn't get results soon they would hire someone else. He had had his men scouring the west country for clues and had even put a watch on the hospital where Mirela's grandmother was a patient, but it had been discovered that she, and the balloonist, were being guarded by police. So there had been no opportunity to question them.

Staring out of the window over the rooftops, Bruno was trying to formulate a plan of action, when the door to his suite burst open and Anton hurried in waving a newspaper.

"Got them at last, Boss," Anton enthused. "Here, read this article, no wonder we couldn't find them, they'd escaped to the Channel Isles."

Bruno snatched the newspaper from Anton, and sitting on his bed, he read the article avidly with a new hope beginning to flicker within him. The article described how Chris and Mirela, travelling with an uncle, had booked passage on a schooner bound for the Channel Isles. The schooner had hit bad weather, but although being badly damaged, had managed to stay afloat and had been towed, by the Jersey Lifeboat, back to safety.

Bruno sprang off the bed and began to pace furiously around the room. After several minutes he stopped and turned to Anton, who was lounging in an easy chair.

"Right Anton. Get in touch with the airport and book flights to Jersey as soon as possible. I'm going to make some phone calls. This Joseph Dudley, the girl's uncle, he was responsible for shooting Gino, but for him we would have bagged the two children by now. I should have him eliminated, but we can't risk MI5 getting involved."

Anton stood and made his way to the door, but hesitated, then turned to Bruno. "I'm not questioning your authority boss, but do you mind if I ask a question?"

Bruno frowned. He was not used to his men asking questions. Especially Anton, who's military past made him an ideal person for following orders without question.

"What's on your mind Anton? What is it you want to know?"

"Well – it's just that we seem to be concentrating more on capturing the two kids, when we might have had better luck with the father. He is the one who has the formula and although he is guarded at all times, we could put a plan in place to overcome his protection and take him."

"I don't pay you to question what I do, Anton, or how I do it," lectured Bruno. "But I will tell you this. There is something very special about the boy which makes it essential that we take him instead. He did seem at first to be the easier target, but the young girl seems to have unusual influence over him and a strange awareness of how to avoid being caught. Now go and book our flights, there's a good chap, and don't ask so many questions."

***

Corbiere Lighthouse, on the western side of the island, presented one of the most spectacular views on Jersey. The downhill approach to the causeway afforded one the opportunity to study the scene. The whitewashed lighthouse surrounded by the now exposed, perilous rocks, with the blue sea stretching to the horizon, brought gasps of pleasure from Chris and Mirela. They alighted from the car close to a Second World War German bunker, a reminder of a less happy time, when the islands were occupied by Axis forces.

As they walked across the causeway, the sea had not fully ebbed and the water lapped over the edges and wet their feet. On each side the red granite rocks had formed pools when the tide had receded, which the children took note of to explore later, should they get the opportunity. As they approached the lighthouse the lantern suddenly came on as though to welcome them. This was a surprise to the children because it was not yet dusk. Joseph led the way up the steps to the door where they were met by the keeper.

Later, after they had eaten and been shown where they would sleep, the keeper, James Le Mont, gave them a tour of the lighthouse and a brief history of the structure. Completed in 1874, it was built entirely of concrete rather than the traditional stone block work. Many lighthouses which had been built from stone required complex arrangements of interlocking blocks to prevent the sea from eroding, and finally demolishing, man's handiwork. Corbiere, on the other hand, had no chinks or fissures for the sea to probe in search of weakness, so it had withstood the test of time without apparent difficulty. With a total elevation above the sea of 135 feet and a tower height of sixty-two feet, Corbiere is not among the giants of the lighthouse world. The lantern, which can be seen at a range of eighteen miles, in good conditions, is fired by paraffin and requires constant attention by the keepers. There is also a foghorn which sounds when the fog comes down. The mournful tones of the foghorn are referred to as *la vache de Corbiere* – the Corbiere cow. Corbiere itself means: the place where crows congregate.

***

Mirela awoke suddenly. Something had disturbed her sleep. Still feeling exhaustion from their experience onboard *The Dolphin*, they had crawled into bed early and she had slept soundly for several hours, but what was it that had disturbed her? She knuckled the sleep out of her eyes and looked around her. The moon filtering through the window provided a pale, ghostly light that made it possible to distinguish Chris's sleeping form lying in the bed across the room. She couldn't quite get used to the rooms not having any corners, it seemed strange and unnatural. She got out of bed and went to the window. The tide was high, and the sea swirled restlessly around the base of the lighthouse. The causeway was completely covered now, as were the jagged rocks that they had seen earlier. On the distant shoreline, the German bunker crouched menacingly, as though waiting for its past masters to appear and occupy the islands again.

She jumped involuntarily when she suddenly heard a voice. She turned from the window and listened, it was Chris talking in his sleep again. She crept to his bedside, the better to hear what he was saying. This had happened several times before, but she couldn't understand his mutterings. It sounded very much like a complex set of maths that she was quite unfamiliar with. She listened for some minutes until he went quiet, then she made her way back to her bed, but before she got there a sudden loud bellow erupted from close by. Mirela froze to the spot, terrified, her hand flew to her mouth stifling a scream, then as the sound died away she ran back to Chris's bed and flung herself under the bedclothes trembling. Chris, disturbed by the commotion, was sitting up staring wide-eyed around him, looking for the source of the noise. Without warning the bellowing sounded again and with a cry of alarm he joined Mirela under the bedclothes.

They lay there hardly daring to breath when Mirela suddenly started to shake. Chris reached out to put a protective arm around her but stopped when he realized she was shaking with laughter. They both sat up and Chris said, nervously, "W-what was that?"

Mirela, spluttering with laughter, said, "It's the Corbiere Cow, fog must have rolled in and the foghorn must have been activated."

They both fell about laughing helplessly until the foghorn startled them again, but this time it only made them laugh all the harder.

After several days, Chris and Mirela started to become accustomed to their strange surroundings. They had recovered from the ordeal of the preceding few days and Joseph was now also looking rested, but there was a watchfulness about him. He monitored every move the children made and was often found sweeping the shoreline with his binoculars, taking in every detail, especially when it was low tide. Joseph would accompany Chris and Mirela when they explored the many rock pools that were close to the causeway. They began to collect many shells and dozens of sea-life species which they studied and wrote about in the exercise books that had been provided for them.

On certain days a car would arrive, organized by Joseph, and they would be whisked away to enjoy a day out somewhere on the island. One of the most unusual places they visited was the underground hospital that had been cut into the hillside and had provided care and treatment for many German soldiers who had been wounded in the fighting. It was a huge construction that stretched far. It had been built by using slave labour, mostly Russian prisoners of war, who had been treated with brutal and inhuman cruelty. It was a chilling place, and as Chris and Mirela explored the wards and the many other chambers lit by sparse, bare, light-bulbs, Mirela began to experience a dreadful feeling of what it must have been like for the prisoners who had lived and died there. Unable to control her sensitive mind it seemed to gather sounds and indistinct shadowy scenes from the distant past. She could hear the sound of men digging frantically, while a whip cracked and each time a cry of pain was heard followed by a coarse oath that urged the prisoners to work harder and faster. The sheer feeling of pain, misery and despair felt by the prisoners almost overwhelmed her, she was hurried to the exit by Chris and Joseph where she was able to gradually calm her mind and recover.

One day, while Chris and Mirela were studying the sea creatures that they had collected in their jars and were entering observation notes into their books, Mirela asked, "Chris?"

"Yes?"

"I heard you talking in your sleep again last night, but I couldn't understand what you were saying." She frowned. "It seemed to have something to do with school. There were a lot of numbers involved. You seem to be having this dream quite a lot. Do you remember any of it?"

Raising his head from his work he stared thoughtfully out of the window, chewing the top of his pencil, then he looked at Mirela and shrugged. "I can vaguely remember a string of numbers that seem to keep popping up in my mind, but other than that, no I don't remember the dreams."

After a while they returned to their writing, both appearing to have forgotten the subject they had been talking about, but Chris was uneasy. He respected Mirela's ability and wondered whether she sensed that he was not being honest with her. She had herself experienced some horrendous dreams, but a lot of it was her sensitivity to danger and also her being able to see what could happen in the future. Chris knew that he had an extraordinary memory, but he had the feeling that a part of his mind was blocking something that he was not really allowed to access, and that something was seeping into his subconsciousness in the form of dreams. They continued with their writing until supper, when they were called down to the kitchen where they each collected a cup of cocoa and everyone gathered in front of the fire to talk of the day's events.

A wind had got up which was dashing the waves over the

exposed rocks and it moaned and wailed piteously around the lighthouse. Chris, gazing out of the window, shivered involuntary and asked, "Has anything strange ever happened in this lighthouse, Mr Le Mont, anything scary or ghostly that people remember?"

"No, there is very little to tell about Corbiere. With it being so close to land there has always been help at hand in an emergency, but not so with The Flannan Isle Lighthouse." He settled back in his chair and stared into the fire as though searching for the truth to the mystery amongst the glowing coals. "There were three lighthouse-keepers on Flannan Isle which was approximately twenty miles from the Outer Hebrides, western Scotland. Thomas Marshall, James Ducat and Donald Macarthur. The mystery began on the night of 15 December 1900, when a squall blew up in the vicinity of the island."

"We know about squalls, don't we Mirela?" Chris announced, interrupting David Le Mont. "We were caught in one when we were aboard *The Dolphin*. We thought the ship was going to sink. It was terrifying."

David Le Mont nodded knowingly. "Yes! Joseph told me about what happened in the Channel. Squalls can appear so quickly and are so violent they can catch seafarers unaware. Now, where was I, oh yes – the crew of two passing ships reported that they had seen no guiding light from the Flannan Isle lighthouse, and bad weather delayed the relief ship, *The Hesperus* from sailing. It was not until Boxing Day that the supply ship was able to sail out to the islands with the relief keeper, Joseph Moore. Things were eerie on the lighthouse island. There was no welcoming committee from the three men (who would normally have been outside to greet them), no provisions boxes had been put out to be re-stocked, and the flag wasn't up on the flagstaff. *The Hesperus* moored in silence, and Joseph Moore headed for the lighthouse, calling out as he headed towards it. Myth has it that when Joseph Moore first opened the main door, three strange birds flew out, and, when the lighthouse tower was searched, odd strands of seaweed were found on the stairs and in the little cubbyhole where the lighthouse logbook was kept. Other than that, inside the lighthouse nothing looked out of order. The lamps were trimmed, the beds were unmade as if the men had just got up, the washing-up done, cold ashes in the grate, and the clocks had all stopped. It was found that two sets of outdoor gear were missing, and only one set of oilskins remained, which meant one of the men had gone out without his protective weather gear on, something that would have been virtually unheard of. One of the oddest things of all was all three men had left the light unattended, which went against the rules laid down by the Northern Lighthouse Board. A search was made of the island itself. At the west landing stage, they found extraordinary damage. Iron railings were bent out of shape and the iron railway, by the path, was completely wrenched out of the concrete. The conclusion was that the damage had been caused during a terrible storm. The lighthouse had no wireless communication and its only way to send a message to the outside world was by setting a series of semaphore-style balls on posts which could be seen by the Hebrides on a good day."

"What is semaphore Mr Le Mont?" asked Mirela curiously, when the lighthouse-keeper paused in his narration to puff several times on his pipe to keep it alight.

"Semaphore is a method of sending messages by positioning signs or flags in certain ways, so they can give a message over visible distances. The navy uses this method by having trained signallers, holding a flag in each hand, and positioning the flags at certain angles around his person to send signals from ship to ship." Mr Le Mont cocked an eyebrow at Mirela. "Does that answer your question young lady."

"Yes! Thank you. Was there a message left for the supply ship?"

"No! There was no semaphore message, whatever happened must have happened suddenly." Resuming his narrative, Mr Le Mont said, "There have been many explanations offered by many people about what actually happened, but no one knows for sure. According to the logbook, a terrible storm blew up on 12 December that lasted for four days. Sea lashed to fury, waves very high, tearing at the lighthouse. Stormbound, cannot go out. Whatever occurred must have happened on 15 December. The more dramatic explanations are the lighthouse was attacked by sea monsters or aliens. It has even been speculated that a long-boat full of ghosts was seen heading to the island on the night the light went dark. Some have said that long-boat full of ghosts may in fact have been the lighthouse-keepers rowing furiously away. The Northern Lighthouse Board carried out an investigation into the disappearances and concluded that it was most likely that the men had been swept away by a freak wave as they were trying to secure things on the west landing area. That two men got into trouble and the third keeper had dashed outside, in his shirt sleeves, to help them."

Mr Le Mont paused to collect his thoughts. "Superintendent Muirhead, who, in his official report of 8 January 1901, said he visited them as lately as 7 December and had the melancholy recollection that he was the last person to shake hands with them and to bid them farewell."

Later, when Chris and Mirela had climbed into bed and were watching the flicker of light from the lamp as it periodically lit up the window, Mirela remarked, "Those poor men. I really wonder what happened to them, I don't suppose anyone will ever find out. And what about their families, they must have had children. It's just awful to think that they had to grow up without their fathers."

"Yes," agreed Chris. "There seems to be a lot of tragedies connected with the sea. I will never, ever, sail on another ship if I can help it."

Chapter Nineteen

It was low tide and Joseph was at his station, scanning the people walking along the causeway with his binoculars. He would occasionally switch to sweep the shoreline, but his main interest was the visitors crossing to get a closer look at the lighthouse. This meant restricting the time that the children spent at the rock pools. Plans were afoot to move on to a less public place, where the children would be more secure, and where he could spend less time on watch.

Gradually, the visiting numbers dwindled down to the odd couple and he was able to allow Chris and Mirela out on to the causeway, where they were soon immersed in searching for whatever new species the last tide may have washed in. Joseph looked at his watch. The water was beginning to lap at the foot of the causeway and would begin to cover it in thirty minutes. The siren would soon sound as a warning to those visitors still at the lighthouse, or on the causeway, that they had ten minutes to reach the shoreline, or get their feet wet.

Joseph remained at his watch station until the sound of the siren faded away. He looked expectantly for the children to appear as they had been instructed to do when they heard the siren. There had been the sound of a powerboat engine approaching in the last few minutes, and when Joseph had trained his binoculars in that direction, he had recognised that it was clearly classified as an inflatable rescue craft, crewed by three men, probably involved in a coastal training exercise.

The children had still not appeared on the causeway when Joseph left his post and he began to hurry to where he had last seen them. He became aware that the engine of the rescue craft had lessened to a burble and the sound seemed to be coming from around by the rock pool. Suddenly, he was sprinting along the causeway, instinctively realizing that the children could be in danger. Clambering around the red granite rocks that hid the rock pool from the lighthouse, Joseph clearly saw why the children had not appeared.

Mirela was in the clutches of one of the men from the rescue craft, but he was having difficulty keeping hold of her, she was fighting like a wildcat, kicking, scratching and pummelling him to get free. Another burly man was holding Chris firmly over his shoulder and was about to clamber into the rescue craft that was being held close to the rocks by a third man. Joseph rushed at the man holding Mirela, but before he could reach him the man hoisted Mirela above his head and flung her far out into the deepest part of the rock pool, then pulling a gun from his belt he fired at him. Joseph launched himself behind a nearby rock, hearing the bullet ricochet past him as he fumbled for his own weapon. Returning fire, he warily peeped around the rock and saw that his assailant had fled to the inflatable which was being revved-up ready to surge quickly away. Springing from behind the rock he looked frantically for Mirela in the rock pool.

He felt a surge of relief when he saw her break the surface and gasping for breath begin to struggle feebly to the edge. Knowing Mirela was not a strong swimmer he called encouragement to her and shouted that he was going to see what he could do for Chris.

Reaching the water's edge, he could see the craft speeding away about twenty-five yards distant. Knowing he could well hit Chris if he fired at the men, he carefully aimed at the hull of the boat and fired three spaced shots into the bodywork along the port side, in the hope of puncturing the boat so it would flounder. A return volley of shots whistled overhead as Joseph ran back to the pool to see that Mirela had struggled almost to the edge, and as he pulled her out he hugged her to him murmuring how very brave she was.

Joseph sat her in a shelter of rocks and promised her he would be back very soon. He ran to the place where he could see if the inflatable was still in sight and was amazed to see the boat wallowing in the choppy sea. He mentally blessed the time he had spent at target practice and watched while the occupants bailed frantically to try and stay afloat. Suddenly, a small figure, detaching itself from the group, dived overboard and began to swim away from the stricken craft. Joseph knew the swimmer was Chris. He had taken advantage of the chaotic situation and decided the time was now or never.

Another figure left the sinking craft and started swimming after Chris. Joseph watched the progress of the swimmers, ready to swim out to assist Chris should he begin to tire. The man seemed to be gaining on Chris. The choppy seas were taking their toll on whatever strength Chris had left. He still had about twenty yards to swim when Joseph plunged into the sea and swam to where he was starting to flounder. Reaching Chris, he grabbed hold of him and set off, swimming strongly, back to the causeway.

Reaching the shore, they both lay gasping for breath for a short while, then Joseph told Chris where to find Mirela while he scanned the waters for the man who was in pursuit of Chris. There was no sign of anyone in the water, so he surmised the swimmer must have returned to the inflatable to be picked up by another boat that was visibly ploughing its way towards the capsized group. Re-joining Chris and Mirela, Joseph held on to them tightly as they made their way along the now knee-deep, swirling water of the causeway to the lighthouse, where they were met with towels and blankets by a worried looking James Le Mont.

Later, having dried out and recovered somewhat from their unexpected dipping, they sat with hot drinks while Joseph stared moodily out to sea, thinking about the kidnappers who seemed able to find them where ever they were.

"They are obviously a highly organized group, who have good information and plenty of resources, which makes them unpredictable and dangerous. They could possibly be linked to a group from outside the UK," said Joseph, thoughtfully. "Your father must be too well guarded for them to go after him, so they are concentrating upon you, Chris, the softer option, with intent to put pressure upon your parents to hand over the formula they want so badly."

Joseph paced the floor, deep in thought. "I must contact one of my colleagues and have him find us a safer and more secure place to stay. We will need guards. It is essential that we take more precautions now that the threat has followed us to Jersey and you children remain in such danger."

The following days spent at the lighthouse proved to be less adventurous for Mirela and Chris. Some of the magic of staying in such an unusual place had gone, to be replaced by feelings of uncertainty. They were reluctant to stray far along the causeway, preferring instead to sit on the steps below the entrance to the lighthouse, watching the visitors arrive and depart.

One day, Chris looked at Mirela and asked, "You didn't seem to have any foreboding about what was about to happen to us this time Mirela. Could it be that your special gift may be waning?"

Mirela looked at Chris with troubled eyes. Then looking off into the distance, she said, "It's been bothering me that I didn't sense the approach of danger this time, and I don't know why. Perhaps being on the island, and staying at the lighthouse with Joseph guarding us, gave me a sense of security that lulled me into thinking that we were out of reach of the men who wanted to take us," she paused and held her head as though listening, her eyes unfocused.

Suddenly, her face lit up with a joyous smile and her voice rose as she exclaimed. "But there is someone who may be able to answer those questions for me. I sense that my grandmother, Rosanna, has arrived on the island and will be with us shortly. Come, let's find Joseph and tell him the good news."

The water had barely drained from the causeway when the small figure appeared, holding her long dress up as she picked her way carefully between the pools that still remained. As soon as Mirela recognised her grandmother's familiar figure, she ran splashing towards her, closely followed by Chris. They descended upon Rosanna with damp enthusiasm, hugging her so tightly that she had to give up trying to keep her dress dry and returned their unrestrained show of affection with laughing protests.

"Heavens children, put me down, you've mobbed and soaked me enough. Now, take me to see Joseph before I drown."

Joseph smiled at Rosanna's dishevelled appearance and greeted her tenderly.

"Welcome to Jersey, Rosanna. It's good to see you again, I trust you have fully recovered from your injuries enough to be here."

"Yes! I am almost fully recovered, Joseph, and looking forward to joining you in watching over the children. Now, tell me what has been happening and what future plans you have?"

Chapter Twenty

The arrangements to move the children out of the lighthouse to a new secret destination were complete. The vehicle that delivered provisions to the lighthouse was to be used to smuggle the four of them to a property in the parish of St Ouen. The driver would take his usual delivery route around the island, not making any changes which could cast suspicion upon his movements. He would be making genuine deliveries to customers and finish on the west of the island where the four escapees were bound. Conditions were cramped for the four as they lay behind the boxes and bags of provisions, but eventually they reached their destination and the van backed up to the garage to unload the provisions that they themselves would need for their time there. They lay quietly, waiting for the signal to leave the van. When it came, they darted into the garage, closed the door behind them and entered their new quarters with sighs of relief.

The premises were surprisingly spacious for a bungalow and the limited view, through drawn curtains revealed low sand hills that led to a distant shore. As they became more familiar with their new surroundings, it was discovered that a high-ranking German officer had also made the bungalow his home during the occupation of the island. More searching revealed a staircase that led down to a large basement and, quite surprisingly, the discovery of a strong metal door that provoked many a wild guess of, why it was there and where it might lead.

Later, enquiries by Joseph revealed that the western side of the island was where the occupying German forces would have expected the allied forces to have landed to retake Jersey in 1944. That was why it had been so heavily fortified. It seemed the area was honeycombed with tunnels, which would have linked up command posts with communication to the weapon sites that would have provided a powerful defence for that part of the coast. The door in the basement obviously led to a tunnel that would have enabled the officer, living there then, to reach his command post quickly in an emergency. Such historical events fascinated Chris and he began to spend time writing a journal about the occupation of the island. It would only be a matter of time before the temptation to explore the tunnel proved to be irresistible to him.

The security arrived almost as soon as they moved in. There were three of them, well-armed, trained and efficient. Each man had an eight-hour shift and held full responsibility for the security of the premises and the safety of each person in the house. Being followed everywhere by one of the security men was a novelty at first to Mirela and Chris, but the restrictions soon became irksome when they found their freedom was suffering and their time spent running free on the beach was limited. The children found the men friendly enough and would laugh and joke with them, but they would often become stern and order them to do things that they didn't want to do, like not straying too far away, or cutting short a visit or an activity that they were enjoying. Constantly on the alert, the guard would steer them away from groups of people, or from a place that they found interesting, where they had paused to watch some pastime or a game being played. Sometimes Joseph would take over from the man on duty and accompany Mirela and Chris on their beach visits. He would not be such a stickler about how long they would spend on the beach and would join them in their fun and games, watching over them as they swam and surfed and enjoyed themselves as children should.

The opportunity to explore what was behind the door in the basement came one evening when Chris discovered that someone had forgotten to lock it. He had ventured a short distance into the tunnel, but without some form of light he knew he would be stumbling about in the dark. So, he returned to the basement, closed the door and went to his room where he collected a torch and other things that he thought he would need for a return visit to the tunnel. When he informed Mirela of what he intended to do, she was also curious about the tunnel and said she would go with him, although she was apprehensive about being caught by the one of the security men.

"We will be alright if we are quiet," said Chris. "The guards stick mainly to the kitchen, listening to the radio and making coffee. We can sneak past the kitchen and down the basement steps in between their house patrol times. A good time would be about five thirty in the morning. That will give us about two hours to find out what is down there, don't forget to bring a torch."

At five thirty a.m., Chris and Mirela met in the hall between their two rooms and snuck past the kitchen, where they could hear the radio playing, and down the steps to the basement. Chris held his breath while he tried the door handle, hoping that whoever had left the door unlocked had not returned to lock it. Stepping into the tunnel, they closed the door behind them and switched on their torches. The tunnel was surprisingly large and reinforced, stretching well beyond the limited beams of their torches. They began to walk slowly along the tunnel, occasionally casting their torchlight upon the walls each side of them as they walked. The air smelt stale and musty and there was an eerie silence that picked up the slightest sound and increased it two-fold. Chris had brought a small compass which showed that they were travelling due west towards the sea.

After a short distance, they became more confident and picked up the pace and soon came to a junction that headed north west. After a short discussion Chris decided they should continue along the main tunnel and leave the one that travelled north west for another time. Soon, they came to a spacious area where there were two rooms that had been used as living quarters and a third room that had probably acted as a command area. Broken and splintered bunk beds lay in one room and a dust covered table and chairs lay in the other. The third room held a scarred-topped desk with drawers pulled open spilling folders and sheets of papers everywhere. A narrow iron staircase led upwards from the command area. Chris climbed the staircase to a metal doorway which would not budge when he tried to open it. Giving up, he descended the stairs to find Mirela rummaging through the desk drawers.

"I don't think there is anything of interest here, Chris, just lots of papers written in German," remarked Mirela.

They wandered around looking at the writings and the drawings of helmeted German soldiers that adorned the walls, accompanied by the dreaded swastika symbols that seemed to be emblazoned everywhere. There was an oppressive silence that was a little unnerving and it gave a feeling that just by being there they could perhaps awaken the dreadful events of the past. Mirela's torch was beginning to dim a little, so the decision to return to the basement was taken. They made their way quickly along the tunnel, past the junction that led north west, when Chris's torch also began to dim.

Suddenly, Mirela stopped and clutched Chris's arm in a vice like grip. Turning, he shone his torch on Mirela and was about to ask her what was wrong when he noticed her face had paled and her eyes were large and frightened as she stared back along the tunnel.

"There's someone down here with us," she whispered. "I can feel its presence behind us, it's coming fast."

The footsteps could be heard clearly now, striding along, heavy-footed, becoming louder as they drew nearer. Then suddenly, they stopped, and silence descended once more. Mirela still held on to Chris's arm and he could feel her hand trembling and hear her breath coming in gasps as the dread within her mounted. With thudding heart, Chris directed the beam of his torch back along the tunnel, and there, almost at the limit of the torch's weakened beam, was a vision that the world had come to despise and fear. A vision that represented merciless cruelty, brutality and utter horror.

The figure stood, almost filling the space behind them. The black helmeted head with the white SS markings upon it. The pale, harsh, cruel face beneath the helmet with dark fathomless eyes. The black uniform with trousers tucked into gleaming black jackboots completed the nightmarish image. Time seemed to stand still as they remained frozen to the spot with fear. The scream that had remained locked within Mirela suddenly released itself and the piercing sound filled the tunnel, breaking the spell.

Mirela dropped her useless torch and still clutching Chris's arm, dragged him with her as she raced back along the tunnel. As they ran, Chris's torch threw erratic flashes of light around the tunnel with barely enough illumination to light the way back. Gasping for breath they tumbled into the basement and closed the door firmly behind them. They pause to regain their breath and then as silently as possible they made their way back to their rooms without alerting the security guard. Their sleep that dawn was disturbed often, as they imagined with dread what would happen if the phantom appeared to take revenge for trespassing in his lair.

***

Felix Gordeaux added another address to the short list he already had. That was about all of the houses that he needed to take a closer look at, three in all. He needed to leave out the places that were used as holiday homes and examine the places that were occupied by strangers, then report back to the man who had hired him. He was parked not far from the bungalow that he suspected was the kind of place he had been instructed to look for, and what's more, he had visited the property in times gone by. He looked out of the rain-streaked windscreen of his van, recalling again what had happened to change his routine so much.

Slightly built and quick of movement, his pointed features with thin lips hiding crooked teeth and his small hazel eyes, lent him an air of furtiveness that made people wary of him. He had been calling at houses selling seasonable vegetables and fruit; that had been his living since the war had ended. One day he had been stopped by a car that had come alongside and flagged him down. Two burly men had approached and asked him if he was Felix Gordeaux. Warily, thinking that they might be the police, he nodded and waited nervously for them to tell him what they wanted.

The blonde one, the taller of the men, had regarded him with cold blue eyes and began to speak with a slight foreign accent.

"We would like you to be at the La Saline Slip at 10 a.m. tomorrow morning where you will be met by a person who has a need to hire you for your knowledge. You will be well-rewarded for any information you can provide and any work you carry out will bring an added bonus." The man leaned closer and continued menacingly "Be on time and do not make us have to come and look for you."

Felix again nodded his head dumbly and watched as the men climbed back into their car and sped off.

The next morning, he had arrived at the La Saline Slip car park in his van and parked up to await contact. An unexpected tap on his window had made him jump and he looked up to find the man with the cold blue eyes beckoning to him. Climbing out of his cab he was led to a vehicle parked a short distance away, where he was invited to join another person seated in the rear of a car. Seating himself, he was greeted with a handshake and a warm smile by a man who introduced himself as Bruno.

"Thank you for coming, Felix. I have been told that you have a good knowledge of the area of St Ouen. What I need is for you to take note, while doing your rounds, of any strangers who may have moved into any one of the properties in the area." Bruno paused and looked directly at Felix. "I am aware that you collaborated with the Germans during the war, and you learnt certain ways of obtaining information that you passed on to your masters for payment. I am not in the least bit concerned about your past. All I want is for you to do the same for me and I will pay you well. What do you think? Can you do this for me?"

Felix had paid a visit to the property that he suspected Bruno would be most interested in. A man had come to the door in answer to his knock, and while Felix had been going over the list of items he had for sale, the man had examined him carefully and had looked searchingly beyond the approaches to the bungalow. The man was dressed in a business suit and Felix was sure that the bulge under his coat was a shoulder holster that carried a gun. The man was about to refuse purchasing any of the items that Felix had mentioned, when a small woman had appeared and had told the man that they did have need of fruit and vegetables. She had purchased a quantity that would have been enough for five or six people. It was time to meet with Bruno and inform him of what he had learnt.

This time the meeting was held in a hotel suite. After Felix had informed Bruno of what he had learnt, he displayed an interest in the woman who had bought the fruit and vegetables and asked for a description.

"She was a small woman, dressed in a long, ankle length dress. She had olive skin, piercing dark eyes and her hair was parted in the middle and pulled back into a bun," Felix recalled.

"Hmmm, it looks like Rosanna survived the balloon crash and has returned to help safeguard the children," murmured Bruno. Then he added, "You have done well Felix. All I want you to do now is to show my men where the property is and then leave the rest to them. Here is your payment, you can leave now."

Felix accepted the bulky envelope and stuffed it into his pocket, then hesitantly, he said, "I think you will find that I can be of further use to you, because I have more information about the property you are interested in. There is another way of entering the house other than using the front entrance. I discovered it during my visits there when I worked for a colonel who was involved in intelligence gathering during the occupation." Felix paused to see what kind of reaction he was getting and was encouraged to see that he had Bruno's full attention.

"Go on," said Bruno abruptly.

"There are underground connecting tunnels all over St Ouen that the Germans could have used to great effect in the event of them having been invaded. Several of the houses used by high-ranking German officers were used as command posts and were connected directly by tunnels to the gun-sites, so that the officers could quickly be where they would be of most use. The property that you are interested in has such underground connections."

Bruno was now leaning forward in his seat totally focused on what Felix was telling him. There was an excited look on his face when he asked, "Do you know where the tunnel leads to from the property?"

"Yes!" said Felix. "When the Germans left I hid in the tunnels and got to know my way around quite well. There was lots of abandoned equipment and stacks of paperwork, some of it looked quite important. I also found maps of the tunnel network which were very useful to me. Later, when I was arrested, I was able to negotiate a lesser sentence when I gave the allies all the important paperwork that I had collected, but I kept the map of the tunnels for my own use."

Bruno stroked his chin thoughtfully. This news was of

tremendous value and to think it had fallen into his hands in such a simple way.

"Would you be willing to guide me and my men through the tunnels to the house where the woman Rosanna is staying?" he asked. "You will be well rewarded if you do this, but now you must describe to me the construction of the door that leads from the tunnel into the house, and its locking mechanism."

Felix hesitated. He hadn't expected to be asked to guide the group through the tunnels and he was reluctant to do so. He had once looked upon the network of tunnels to be his domain. He had wandered throughout the underground system as he pleased, but now there was something down there, something frightening, something he didn't want to meet and confront. He had had a brief encounter, a glimpse of the entity, and he had fled the tunnels ever since. However, if he was to be the guide he would be with a group and they would only be down there for a short time. The payment would be worth the risk, he thought, and I won't tell them of what I saw down there. They will probably just laugh at me anyway.

Bruno took Felix's hesitance as a way of increasing the payment he would receive.

"All right, Felix," said Bruno, with impatience. "I will double your payment if you will guide us through the tunnels to the bungalow."

"Okay. I will do what you ask, but there is no need to discuss the door's construction," Felix added, a smug look appearing on his ferret-like features. "You see, I also have a bunch of keys which have been coded with typical German thoroughness and I am sure that one of them must fit the door in question."

Chapter Twenty-One

One day in early September, Mirela walked with her grandmother along the quiet lanes close to the bungalow. The hot days of summer had all but gone, leaving the warm mellow days of early-autumn to caress the land and to ripen the fruits for harvesting. Mirela had been silent for some time. Usually, she talked non-stop when she was in her grandmother's company and Rosanna was concerned that perhaps she was worrying about something she found hard to discuss.

"Heavens child! I've not known you to be so quiet for so long. Is something bothering you?" Mirela stopped and looked up, there was a tightness to her mouth and a look of uncertainty in her eyes that worried Rosanna. She put a comforting arm around her shoulder and said, "Tell me Mirela. Tell me why you are so troubled."

"Oh Grandma! When will we ever be safe again?" Mirela cried. "There seems no end to the places we must escape to. These people keep chasing us, and sooner or later they will succeed in taking Chris. I'm so afraid for him. When we were almost taken at the lighthouse I did not sense that there was danger when I should have. I didn't feel the foreboding that I had sensed before when something bad was going to happen. I think I am losing my power of intuition."

"There, there, my child," murmured Rosanna, hugging Mirela

tightly. "You and Chris have been through so much that it is only natural you would question what the future holds. As for your gift, you are still very young, and it will take time for you to reach the height of your perceptive abilities." Rosanna held Mirela's face in her hands and looked deep into her eyes and said, "You are an extraordinary young lady, and you will grow and become a more extraordinary young woman and I will be at your side always."

Mirela kissed her grandma and smiled. "I missed you so much when you weren't here with me and I missed your guidance even more. Let's go back and I will help you with the evening meal."

Linking arms, they quickened their step as they walked back to the bungalow and with every step Mirela's uncertainties seemed to lift and float away on the early evening breeze.

During the evening meal, Rosanna noticed that Joseph didn't seem to be eating much. He would eat a morsel or two, then push the rest of the food around his plate leaving much of it uneaten. He had been suffering severe headaches for some days now and looked flushed and feverish. He stood and excused himself saying he wasn't feeling too well and that he was going to lie down. Later, concerned that Joseph may need to see a doctor, Rosanna went to his room to check on him and was alarmed to see that his condition had worsened. He was soaked in sweat and thrashing about, muttering incoherently. She immediately called a doctor who asked her for the patient's symptoms and promised he would be at the bungalow as soon as possible. An hour later, Joseph was being whisked to hospital in an ambulance with Rosanna accompanying him.

Arriving at the hospital, Joseph was placed in the emergency ward where blood tests were taken. Rosanna was then informed that it was thought that Joseph was suffering from a severe attack of malaria. He was very ill, and it was essential to try and bring his temperature down, which was dangerously high. Rosanna recalled that Joseph had served some time in the far east during the war where he must have contracted it.

He had obviously not received the correct treatment at the time to have suffered another attack. It would be difficult to meet the same standard of security without him. Meanwhile, she would have to inform the guard back at the bungalow that she would have to remain at the hospital to await news of any change in Joseph's condition.

The activity at the bungalow had not gone unnoticed. The man who had his binoculars trained upon the bungalow lay on a slight rise, hidden amongst gorse bushes. He noted how many people had left the premises in the ambulance and hurriedly passed on the information using the radio link he had with him.

Bruno, receiving the information passed on by Anton, had recognised the opportunity that had presented itself and realized it was not to be missed. He proceeded to put his men on standby, with instructions to be ready to move at a moment's notice. This time he intended to lead the group himself. Felix would show the way through the tunnels while he followed, and Anton and four other men would fall in behind. Weapons would be issued with instructions to only shoot if there was armed resistance.

Felix met Bruno and his men at La Saline Slip at two a.m. and they drove to the Moltke gun emplacement at Les Landes, where they were to enter the tunnel system. Bruno waited impatiently while Felix sorted through the bunch of keys looking for the right one. Finding it, he inserted it into the lock and was surprised when it turned so easily. As soon as the door opened, Felix stepped aside and allowed the black-clad, well-armed group to clamber down the iron staircase to the lower level where they gathered to do some last-minute checks, before continuing their passage through the tunnels.

Felix had described the state of the bunker and Bruno had thought it would be an ideal place to keep the children after they had been abducted. There were a number of rooms with strong doors and the furnishings appeared to be all in one piece. Perhaps this bunker had been used by the allies when they had explored the tunnels.

Anyway, they would only need it for about forty-eight hours, then they could abandon it.

Soon they were ready to move. Felix took the lead, lighting the way with a powerful torch, with Bruno following and his men bringing up the rear. Felix was not happy being up at the front. He had broken out in a nervous sweat, dreading what would happen if they were to meet up with whatever else was down there.

Keeping up a steady pace, they arrived at the door to the basement of the bungalow without incident. Felix inserted a key into the lock, turned it, and pushed the door open carefully to reveal an empty basement. As soon as they had all gathered in the basement, Bruno turned to his men giving instructions in a low voice.

"Anton, you take two men and take care of the guard. After you have done that, break a rear window and the front door, from the outside, to make the police think that we entered that way." Bruno turned to the other two men. "You two come with me and help me find the children, we will tie them up if necessary. We will meet down here again when you have all finished. Right! Go." Turning to Felix, he said, "You stay down here and be prepared to lock the door behind us when we leave."

Mirela woke from the dream that seemed to have been bothering her a lot lately. It was so frightening that she had woken screaming several times, which had resulted in Chris and the guard rushing to her room to see what was wrong. Even during the day there was the constant feeling of approaching danger and it all seemed to be connected with the tunnels. She wasn't sure if the dreams were a reaction to the experience she and Chris had suffered when they had been confronted by the ghostly soldier, or whether there was another danger that was about to appear.

They had reported to the guard that the basement door was unlocked, but he had said that Joseph had kept the key on his person and it was probably with him at the hospital. Rosanna had noticed the key amongst Joseph's possessions and had given it to the guard on her last visit to the bungalow. Knowing that the bungalow was now secure had not helped Mirela feel safer. She had been seeking Chris's company more than ever, so that she didn't have to be alone in her room.

***

The basement stairway led up to a hallway where Anton paused with his men. They could hear a radio playing softly in a room off to their right. Anton crept quietly towards where the music was coming from and stopped at a door that was slightly ajar. Counting to three he burst through the door, followed closely by his men, and pointing his gun at a man sitting at a table, called for him not to move and to raise his hands. The guard, young and lean, reacted swiftly, flung himself to the right and pulled his handgun from a shoulder holster in one fluid motion, firing off a quick shot at the intruders. Anton ducked as he felt the bullet crack past his head and returned fire, hitting the guard who slumped over clutching his chest and slowly collapsed in a heap on the kitchen floor.

Awakened from his sleep by the gunfire, Chris leapt out of bed and flinging his bedroom door open he rushed out into the hall. He was immediately grabbed by Bruno who had been about to enter his room. Chris shouted with fright and struggled to get free, but Bruno held him firmly and hissed angrily.

"Keep still, or I will be forced to hurt you. Just keep quiet and you won't be harmed." Then turning to his companions, he said, "Let's find the girl quickly, we don't have too much time."

Chris was pulled, and half dragged down the hall to the next room. Immediately they opened the door and switched on the light. Various missiles were flung at them and a girl's high-pitched voice screamed at them to get out. Cursing, Bruno quickly tied Chris's hands and feet and left him in the hall to go and check on Anton's progress, leaving the two men to deal with Mirela.

"Sorry boss, I was forced to shoot the guard when he pulled a gun on us," Anton apologised with a shrug.

"Can't be helped," Bruno said ruefully, looking down at the guard. "He took his chance and paid the price. See to the front door and the rear window and we'll meet in the basement when you're done."

Felix stepped through the door in to the tunnel. Everyone else had left the basement and were waiting for him. He turned the key locking the door, tested it, then pushed his way to the front of the group to take up the lead. The rope around the feet of the children was removed and a short line attached to the bonds securing their hands. As the group started to move along the tunnel with Felix lighting the way, both Chris and Mirela dragged their feet reluctantly, not willing to cooperate with their capturers, but the line was tugged violently, hurting their wrists and almost making them trip and fall. Chris decided to keep pace with the hurried movement of the group until perhaps another chance to be disruptive cropped up. As the group moved along the tunnel, Felix didn't realize he wasn't the only one to be fearful about what else was down there. Mirela peered ahead, uncertain if a sudden appearance of the phantom soldier would prove to be an advantage to them. In the resulting confusion there might be a chance to slip away and escape along the branch tunnel.

Eventually, they arrived back at Moltke emplacement without mishap, where Bruno gave instructions to his men to clean up the area and to lock the children in the cells which had previously been used to store ammunition. The generator had proved to be in good working order and was providing adequate low voltage lighting.

"I will be leaving you in charge while I meet a colleague at the airport tomorrow," Bruno informed Anton. "I will return here as soon as I can. Work out a signal before I leave, and let me know what it is, so you will know it is me wanting to gain entrance when I return."

Chapter Twenty-Two

Not having had any answer to several phone calls to the bungalow from the hospital, Rosanna felt a deep concerned that all was not well. Thankfully, Joseph was passed the critical stage, his fever had broken, and he was now in a deep, exhausted sleep. She paid off the taxi driver and hurried up the path hoping that her fears would be unfounded. She gasped when she saw the front door hanging from it hinges. Breaking into a run, she entered the hall and called to the security, but only silence greeted her. Hurrying to the kitchen she found the guard lying on the floor, barely breathing. She staunched the blood seeping from the wound as best she could, made him as comfortable as possible and called the emergency services.

When the guard had been rushed to the hospital, the police had questioned her closely and promised that a thorough search would be made to find the people who had attacked the bungalow. Meanwhile, an alert would be broadcast throughout the island for the two kidnapped children. Rosanna did not often despair when faced with difficult situations, but in this instance, she felt quite helpless, not sure of what to do next. She missed Joseph, he would have known what to do, but it would be some time before he was back on his feet again. She composed herself and prepared to try and contact Mirela in the special way that only she and her granddaughter knew. She was sure that if Mirela was still on the island she would know it. For an hour she searched with her mind, but to no avail, so she decided to rest and to try again later. Meanwhile, she would need to contact someone to come and repair the damage to the bungalow, then she would have to visit the hospital to see Joseph again.

Chris and Mirela could talk to each other for short periods when the man guarding them had stepped out of the room. The cells were separated by a lift which had been used to take shells up to the gun above. More than once the guard had caught them talking to each other and had banged the butt of his machine gun against the cell doors and threatened to beat them if they didn't keep quiet. Other men were busy making the area fit to live in, and one was even tinkering with the existing heating system. Cots were moved into the cells and the children were given sandwiches and hot tea. When Mirela asked one of the men what was going to happen to them, he pointedly ignored her, slamming the cell door behind him when he walked away.

The hours seemed to creep by. Chris fell silent and would not respond to anything Mirela said. She doubted that he had fallen asleep. He could often become morose when faced with a difficult situation, so she decided to concentrate in trying to contact her grandmother. Settling into a comfortable position on her cot, she slowly relaxed and went into a deep trance, her mind scanning for the elusive link that would help her identify and harmonize with Rosanna's intellect. She was vaguely aware of a deep rumbling sound that came and went, intruding in her search, but try as she might, there was only the faintest trace that would allow her to know that Rosanna was also searching for her.

Rosanna returned to the hospital when the repairs to the bungalow had been completed. Joseph had awakened from his deep sleep and was sitting up eating a meal. Rosanna was surprised at his seemingly quick recovery but advised him not to rush things and to take a lot more rest. Although he looked worn and tired, Rosanna could see that Joseph's eyes had regained the normal quick alertness about them that they always had. He studied her face and started to question her closely. It wasn't long before she broke down and tearfully told Joseph the bad news of the children's kidnapping and the guard's shooting. His face was grim when he heard all the news and for several minutes he lay back, absorbing what he had been told. Then pressing the alarm to summon the nurse, he threw back the bedclothes, and standing, he stood swaying while he endured a short period of dizziness. The nurse dashed in and lectured Joseph for being out of bed, but he ignored her protestation and asked her to bring his clothes.

"Sorry nurse, I must leave your tender care, I have urgent business to attend to and it won't wait. Now will you get my clothes, or do I walk out of the hospital in my pyjamas?" Joseph immediately started to empty his locker and called to the nurse, "Oh! And while you're at it, please call a taxi to take us to St Ouen."

It took several days of rest before Joseph was well enough to venture out of the bungalow. He took this time to gather as much information as he could about the attack on the bungalow and the kidnapping of the children. They visited the guard hoping that he would be able to talk, but he was still unconscious and his condition critical. The police, although searching the island thoroughly, had not had any reports about the missing children and were widening their search to take in the other islands and the nearby French coast.

Joseph decided to contact a friend whom he had known when they had both worked for MI5. Robert Lomas had made it possible for them to stay when they had first arrived on the island. He could be found helping to organize race meetings at the nearby island racetrack. They arrived in time to witness the first of many races that would be held that day. While Joseph spoke urgently with his friend, Rosanna watched the colourful spectacle of the horses and riders hurtling around the track, endeavouring to be the first past the post. Tiring of watching the horses and riders, Rosanna drifted towards the cafeteria and ordered a pot of tea and scones.

As she enjoyed the refreshments she could still hear the horses galloping by.

The revelation came so suddenly that she almost spilt her tea. The sound of the horses galloping around the track was quite muted in the cafeteria, but it was similar to the mysterious rumbling she had heard when she had tried to contact Mirela. She sat and waited for the next race to begin and listened carefully as the sound of the horses drew near, galloped by, then faded gradually into the distance. To be absolutely sure, Rosanna moved further away from the track so that the sound was more muted, but there was no doubting that the rumbling sound was so similar that she was convinced Mirela must be somewhere in earshot of the racecourse. She hurried to find Joseph and tell him the startling news. She found him at the spot where she had earlier watched the horses go by and he smiled when she appeared.

"My friend, Robert Lomas, has promised to help in any way possible," said Joseph, "But until we find a lead I'm afraid there is not much anyone can do."

Rosanna beamed at him and linked her arm with his as they walked toward the car park. "I think we may have found a possible lead, Joseph. You know about the special gift that Mirela and I share, well..."

When Rosanna had explained to Joseph the possibility of Chris and Mirela being kept somewhere close to the racecourse, he looked at her in amazement and frowned. He did not want to doubt what Rosanna had told him. He understood only too well that the special relationship that Rosanna and Mirela shared was a strange and wondrous thing. But, such a slender clue would lead to the searching of a wide area, and how was he to explain the reason for thinking that the children may be found in that particular area. Joseph sunk into a deep, thoughtful mood and only responded to Rosanna when she placed food and drink before him. Sometime later, he stirred and questioned Rosanna about the damage to the bungalow and where she had found the guard. When Rosanna had answered the questions, Joseph stood and began pacing the floor, turning things over in his mind.

"If the attack had actually begun with breaking down the front door and smashing a window at the back of the bungalow, the guard would naturally have responded to one or the other, and he may well have shot one or two of the intruders. But the guard was found on the floor in the kitchen, which makes me think that he was surprised and was not able to respond before he was gunned down." His eyes darted around the room. "Have we got a torch Rosanna?" he asked. "And can you bring the key to the door in the basement?"

Rosanna followed Joseph down into the basement and unlocked the door that led into the tunnel. Stepping into the tunnel, Joseph swept the torch beam around the floor and grunted in satisfaction.

"There, you see Rosanna, as I suspected, you can see the footprints of many feet in the dust and footprints leading up the stairs into the bungalow. This was where they entered and how they were able to surprise the guard." Joseph shone the torch along the tunnel. "They made it look as if they had entered the bungalow in another way to divert attention away from the tunnels." He stroked his chin thoughtfully. "The children may still be held underground, which is why there haven't been any reports or sightings of them."

Returning to the bungalow kitchen, they began to plan how they would search for the children.

"If you could use your powers to contact Mirela once more, she may be able to give us some helpful information. I will get in touch with my friend Robert, who will be able to tell me where this particular tunnel leads to and where the children may be held. He will also provide us with the backup we will need."

Chapter Twenty-Three

The only way that Chris and Mirela could judge the passing of time was when meals were served to them and the type of food they were given. There was cereal on what they thought was the morning and a type of stew in the evening. On what they judged to be their fourth day of being held in the cells, Chris was taken to a connecting room by two of the guards. When Mirela saw Chris being held firmly by the guards and led away, she demanded to know where he was being taken. When the men ignored her, she battered on the bars of her cell and screamed to be taken with him. Chris looked back at her, his face pale and his eyes wide and frightened. Mirela continued to scream and shout even when they disappeared.

Sinking to her knees she felt a pang of despair as she realized that this time there was no escape, and no one would come to save them. Joseph was too ill to help them, and her grandmother was unable to reach her because she didn't know that they were being kept underground, and their special way of contacting each other was blocked. *Why were they so interested in Chris? Why had they spent so much time hunting him? What did he have that they so desperately wanted?*

Mirela held her head in her hands knowing that there was nothing she could do to help him. She lowered her head and wept tears of helpless frustration, fearing what would happen when the kidnappers had finished with them. Slowly her sobs subsided, and she fell into a numbed depression.

Sometime later, she felt a stirring in her mind. A familiar comforting feeling that she felt whenever her grandmother was about to contact her. Her head snapped up and suddenly she was ready to respond to the connection with Rosanna. Questions poured into her mind that she answered quickly and joyously. She learnt from Rosanna that Joseph had recovered from his illness, and that they were aware that she and Chris were being kept underground. She gave as much information that she could think of, about where they were being held, and the worrying news of Chris being taken away for some unknown reason. Rosanna quickly calmed Mirela's fears and reassured her that now that they knew where Mirela and Chris were being held, plans would be made, and they would mount a rescue as soon as possible.

Chris was led into a room that was dimly lit and sat in a chair. His arms and legs were bound to the chair with tape and a blindfold covered his eyes. He heard the men who had brought him to the room leave, then there was a brief silence. A short time later, two people entered the room and one spoke to him in a low voice.

"Hello Chris. Firstly, I want to reassure you that you and Mirela will not be harmed as long as you cooperate with me. Do I have your agreement on that?"

Chris remained silent. He moved his head towards where the voice had come from. It sounded somehow familiar. He was sure he had heard it before, but where?

"I repeat, will you cooperate with me?" the voice said menacingly, "or do I have to bring your friend Mirela here and subject her to some painful experiences? Will you be able to stand listening to her cries of pain?"

Anger flared in Chris, which succeeded in replacing his fear. How dare this person involve Mirela in his murky activities and threaten to harm her.

"Leave her alone. I will cooperate with whatever you have planned, you monster. I don't know what you want, but it must be something I seem to have for you to have chased us for so long," Chris spat out angrily.

The voice chuckled, "That's the spirit my boy. Now, I am going to give you a sedative to calm you and then I will put you into a hypnotic state, so you will be able to recite the formula that I asked you to remember. All your words will be recorded on tape and when that is done, I will be finished with you. Now, I will roll up your sleeve and you will feel a slight prick. Then, when you are comfortable, I will put you under. There is absolutely nothing to worry about. It will not take long."

There was a murmur of voices and the creaking of a chair as someone sat down. Soon, Chris began to feel a drowsiness taking over him, then the voice, slow and measured, began to induce him to relax and to open the compartment in his mind that contained the formula...

***

The promised help that Robert Lomas said he would give reassured Joseph that there would be enough manpower to take care of whatever opposition there was, if it should come to a fight. Robert met Joseph at the bungalow to discuss what they would do. Joseph was able to give Robert a plausible explanation of how he had discovered where the children were being kept. Robert accepted it and congratulated Joseph upon his investigative abilities, but became a little guarded when he was informed that it was Moltke gun emplacement that was the target. Noticing his hesitancy, Joseph looked questioningly at Robert, who shrugged.

"There have been a number of reports over a period of time of strange goings on at Moltke emplacement. It seems that during the occupation of the islands, a young SS officer, who was badly wounded on the Russian front, was posted to Jersey and put in charge of a group of Russian prisoners who were used to dig the tunnels that now honeycomb most of St Ouen. The young SS officer had had such terrible experiences while in Russia that he had an obsessive hatred of everything Russian. His cruelty knew no bounds. He drove the Russian prisoners mercilessly, whippings, beatings and executions a daily occurrence, he literally worked them to death. Somehow, the prisoners heard about the D-Day landings and knew that if they could survive long enough they would be freed when the allies landed, but it was almost another year before Jersey was freed from occupation. Again, news was passed to the prisoners that liberation was near. The prisoners attacked their guards suddenly and unexpectedly one day and although many of them died in the attack, enough of them survived to overwhelm their hated masters and they massacred them. The young SS officer's body was eventually found hanging from scaffolding in one of the tunnels. He had been tortured over a period of time and cut to pieces."

Robert paused in his narrative to sip some tea and gather his thoughts. "Reports of the ghost of the SS officer haunting the tunnels still come in periodically. There has been no real investigation made and there is no proof that these reports are true, so there you are, for what it is worth, it will not interfere with our arrangements to storm the placement."

Joseph was quiet for a while, then said, "A strange tale, Robert, but if true, the children may be in even more danger than we thought. We must act soon. Now, let's plan our approach and the time when both parties will begin the assault."

***

The door to the room where Chris had been taken opened and Chris was carried out and placed on the cot in his cell. Mirela, grasping the bars to her cell, looked on in alarm.

"What have you done to him?" she shouted furiously at the men. "Does he need a doctor? You will pay for it if he has been harmed."

"Be quiet girl," said one of the men. "He has only been sedated. He will wake up in a few hours' time with nothing worse than a headache."

They walked away down a corridor and out of sight.

"Chris! Chris! Are you alright?" Mirela called out, but there was no answer.

She slumped down on her cot desperately worried as to what had been done to him. Time seemed to drag for Mirela as she waited for Chris to recover. Suddenly, the wonderful, comforting feeling of her grandmother being close by reassured her that they would soon be together.

We are in the tunnel leading from the bungalow. You must guide me to you. Are you alone? How many men are there? I am with Joseph and four armed men. Others will be entering the placement by the surface door. Be brave my child.

Mirela tried to contain her excitement at the thought that she would soon be reunited with her grandmother. Not long now, she thought, with a smile.

Joseph appeared so suddenly it startled Mirela. Holding a large handgun, he put a finger to his lips to signal silence and approached the bars.

"Where are your gaolers?" he whispered.

When Mirela pointed down the corridor, Joseph said, "Call to them and say that you think Chris is choking."

Mirela shouted several times before one of the men appeared asking what all the noise was about.

"It's Chris, I think he's choking. Please help him."

The man called for his companion to fetch the keys and both of them approached Chris's cell. As they unlocked the cell door they were surrounded by Joseph and his men, taking the two men completely by surprise. Joseph took the keys and freed Mirela who rushed to her grandmother and hugged her tightly. The two men were handcuffed and gagged then locked in the cell that Mirela had just vacated. Rosanna hurried to look at Chris. She examined him, but he seemed to be sleeping peacefully, so it was decided to leave him where he was. All this had been done with very little noise, but suddenly there was the crash of the surface door being thrown open and loud shouts as the main party stormed down the stairs to spread out and face the rest of the gang. The gang recovered from the surprise assault quickly, and a fusillade of shots greeted the raiding party.

Anton, a veteran of many battles while serving with the legion, soon realized that they could be trapped in the rooms and ordered his men to break out into the tunnels. Soon a running battle began, with both sides sniping viciously at one another. Being unfamiliar with the layout of the tunnels, Anton cursed when he found that he had led his men down a branch tunnel that was a dead end. He ordered his men to regroup and to get ready to make a counter attack which would hopefully take them back to the Moltke emplacement where they could force an escape to the surface.

As they reloaded their weapons and prepared themselves for the onslaught the lighting suddenly began to flicker and dim. The temperature dropped, and a dark swirling cloud appeared behind them. The gang stared at the cloud, feeling uneasy, and edged back along the tunnel. As the cloud came closer they could see a figure taking shape within the swirling darkness. A figure dressed in the black uniform of the German SS soldier, striding forward, jackboots striking the tunnel floor with resounding echoes. Beneath the black helmet, the eyes blazed out of a pale, cruel face. Before the gang could retreat the cloud enveloped them. Anton was some yards ahead of his men when the cloud hid them from view. He heard them shouting and screaming as they fired their rifles, then it went quiet, except for the thud of jackboots that could be heard advancing with the cloud. Anton fled along the tunnel toward the advancing police group, bullets whipped past him when he appeared, and he threw himself to the ground.

"Don't shoot, don't shoot," he cried. "I surrender. We must get out of here, there is great danger."

The police advanced slowly and disarmed and handcuffed him. He kept casting fearful glances over his shoulder, babbling that they must leave the tunnels and get back to the surface. The police had heard the commotion from up ahead and now that one of the gang had been captured, they wanted to know where the rest of them were. But Anton's agitation that all of his men were gone made them hesitate, unsure what was going on. Robert Dumas sent Anton back to the placement with two men and decided to wait where they were to see what developed.

They didn't have to wait long. They heard the stride of the jackboots approaching with the accompanying swirling black cloud. Robert Dumas had never experienced anything like this before and decided to practice caution in this instance. He ordered his group to retire and return to the placement. Back at the placement Robert Dumas ordered his men to take up defensive positions until he knew what they were dealing with.

Joseph, mystified by what was going on, approached Robert to find out what the situation was. After speaking with his friend, he joined Rosanna and Mirela again, a worried frown on his face.

"The situation is not too clear, but I think we should return to the surface taking Chris with us, I will carry Chris. We must hurry."

Collecting Chris from his cot, the three of them made their way to the staircase that led to the surface, but it was already too late. The temperature dropped suddenly, and the thud of the entity's footsteps became louder with every step. Joseph had barely started to climb the staircase when the door to the surface slammed violently shut. Turning back, they saw the swirling black mass was almost upon them. They retreated to the cell and placed Chris's sleeping form back on the cot. There was no escape. The cell seemed as good as anywhere to shelter, so they closed the cell door and stood watching fearfully as Robert and the police prepared to defend the area.

The footsteps ceased and from within the churning vortex a black helmeted head appeared, the face a deathly white, the fathomless, dark eyes burning with a fascism that knew no pity. The mouth opened and began to roar. "HEIL, HEIL, SEIG HEIL." It thundered and reverberated around the walls, almost deafening those who were there. Eventually, after several minutes, the face and the voice faded to be replaced by the full uniformed figure.

Robert Dumas looked around at his men. They were a good disciplined group, but under these conditions, when they were being confronted by an unbelievable and frightening presence, even the best trained men could crack.

The ghostly figure moved forward and as it advanced, still enveloped in the swirling, pulsing, darkness, objects in its path were hurled violently aside against the walls and against the men holding the defence line. Dumas gave the order to fire and a fusillade of bullets tore into the figure, but the bullets seemed to have no effect. Soon the entity was amongst them, bludgeoning the men with their own rifles and picking them up and smashing them like rag dolls against the blood-smeared walls, while roaring its battle cry.

Joseph, Rosanna and Mirela watched in horror as the entity wrought its fury upon Robert Dumas and his men. Joseph looked desperately around for somewhere to escape, but the darkness had consumed the room and the violence was happening just the other side of the cell door. Rosanna held Mirela close and began to realize that unless they did something to try and defend themselves, this object from hell would not be satisfied until it had destroyed everyone there. She looked into Mirela's frightened eyes and said, "Hold my hands my child, we have work to do. Concentrate with me and allow our minds to blend into one. If we are to survive this day, we must endeavour to challenge this destructive entity and try to make it stop its murderous rampage."

Mirela, trembling, took her grandmother's hands in hers and looked deep into her eyes. Their minds immediately merged into one and as they turned to face their opponent, the power of their combined psyche created a charged orb that hovered about them like a cloak. The concentrated shaft of psyche struck the entity like a blow and staggered it to a stop. The darkness about it flickered uncertainly and the swirling cloud slowed as the figure turned to face where the new attack was coming from. It recovered quickly and once again the figure of the SS soldier disappeared to be replaced by the black helmeted head that filled the tunnel. The dark, burning eyes glared its cold hatred at Rosanna and Mirela as it fought to overcome their combined attack with its own maniacal psyche.

The advantage swayed back and forth as the battle waged. Both Rosanna's and Mirela's eyes had taken on a bright, luminous lustre, but the effort to maintain the force was beginning to tell on them. Perspiration washed their faces and drenched their bodies as the effort to maintain their strength of purpose weakened. Sensing that it was beginning to take the advantage, the entity pressed harder and began to emit a high pitched triumphant note. Rosanna gripped Mirela's hands tighter, a desperate plea urging her granddaughter to join her into making one last gigantic effort.

Mirela would always question where her last source of strength came from as she responded to her grandmother's plea. The luminescence of both Rosanna's and Mirela's eyes glowed brighter and a strength poured into their limbs as their combined psyche became stronger. Again, the combined psychic effort from Rosanna and Mirela struck the entity with such force that it penetrated the entity's psyche to its core.

The face contorted, and the teeth bared into a snarl as the entity fought back to regain the upper hand, but the relentlessly combined psyches of Mirela and her grandmother were too strong. A keening cry of anguish rose to a scream as scenes flickered across the slowly fading pitiless features of the entity. Scenes of a blonde youngster with a group of Hitler Youth, a torchlight parade being saluted by Adolph Hitler, battle conflict and a badly wounded soldier in terrible pain. Slowly, the face faded until all there was left was a bright spot that winked out as the last of the entity's psych vanished, leaving a haunting, forlorn cry echoing through the darkness. The swirling cloud disappeared, receded to a pin-point, then it was gone.

If Rosanna and Mirela had not been holding each other up, both of them would have collapsed, such was their state of exhaustion. Joseph approached them, a look of awe on his face as he led them to the cot, so they could rest. There was movement from Chris at last, he sat up blinking owlishly and looked around at the destruction and at those who were in the cell with him, then asked, with curiosity, "What on earth happened here? Did I miss something?"

Chapter Twenty-Four

Robert Dumas, although shaken, bleeding from a gashed head and limping badly, had survived the ordeal. He took charge of the situation, gathering the walking-wounded, organizing them into groups to care for the more seriously hurt comrades. Word was sent to the emergency services and soon the dead and injured were stretchered away. Police took away the prisoners for interrogation and when Robert could do no more, he sat and talked to Joseph.

"I don't know how I am going to write a report on what happened here," Robert said, pensively. "No one will believe that such death and destruction was caused by a long dead phantom SS soldier."

"Describe it like it was, my friend," replied Joseph. "You have plenty of witnesses who will come forward to corroborate what you say is the truth. Use 'we' a lot to emphasise that you were not alone in the situation. I used to do that quite a lot when I was in the service."

Later, when everyone had recovered from their ordeal and were back at the bungalow, Chris, who seemed none the worse for his experience, was reunited with his parents.

"We are so sorry that we couldn't be with you when you were being hunted by those dreadful people, but we were assured that you were in good hands and being protected by Mirela's family.

The work we were doing was of national importance and the time to complete the work was very short," stated his father.

He reached out to hug his son and his mother took both his hands in hers.

"We will never leave you like that again," she promised. "We will be able to get back to normal family life now that the people who hunted you seem to have got what they wanted."

Chris frowned and looked deeply troubled. "Dad! I told the police that I recognised the voice of the person who drugged and hypnotized me. It was Doctor Previnsky who worked with you at the laboratory."

"I know, son," explained his father. "The police informed us of the treachery of my so-called colleague who lured you to his home under the pretext of wanting you to play with his children. He knew of your gift of being able to remember huge chunks of text, so he took the formula from the safe and on one of your visits to his home he hypnotized you into remembering it. Security was so tight around the laboratories and the living quarters, it was the only way he could be sure of obtaining a copy of the formula for the foreign power that he worked for."

Chris still felt bad about being unaware that he had been the carrier of the formula and it had been taken from him in such an easy way, but when he voiced his concern his father reassured him.

"It's okay, Chris. You see, when we made a copy of the formula, we made a slight alteration to it and placed it in the safe, so that if the formula was stolen, or copied by anyone, it would take them a long time to realize that there was a mistake in the formula which would put them many years behind us in the race to perfect a fuel for interplanetary travel."

This was tremendous news to Chris and it felt as if a great weight had been lifted from him.

"Unfortunately," continued his father. "The boss of the gang, a man named Bruno Fletcher, escaped along with Doctor Previnsky before the raid on the Moltke emplacement took place. But it is hoped that someday they will be found."

***

Chris and Mirela sat in the sand watching the surfers trying to stay upright as the rollers came crashing in to spend themselves upon the beach. Mirela glanced at Chris and remarked, with a smile, "Your aura has much improved since the first time I saw you."

Chris looked wonderingly at Mirela and said, "I can't begin to understand the gift that you and your grandmother share. I only know that I am grateful to you both for all the help you have given me. Without you at my side I doubt if I would have survived."

Mirela was silent for while then she said, "We have shared much, you and I, far more than other people of our age would normally have shared. It has made us aware of the evil intent that exists in some people and the lengths they will go to, to get what they want."

A flight of gulls flew overhead mewling and crying mournfully, and a gust of wind made Mirela shiver, her dress not the normal attire for the chill of late-Autumn. There was an awkwardness between them, both realizing that the time had come for them to go their separate ways and to catch up with lives that had been so rudely interrupted. They had relied so much upon each other for survival, through such difficult times, that there was a reluctance to actually be the first to voice their imminent departure.

Mirela stood, suddenly, and said, "Come, let's not delay," and holding Chris's hand they made their way up the slipway to the picnic area, behind a small beach cafe, where they sat to wait for their respective lifts to turn up.

A van pulled in and drew up to the back door of the cafe. The driver opened the rear doors and proceeded to unload several boxes of vegetables and carry them into the cafe.

Chris nudged Mirela and hissed, "Look who's turned up."

Mirela turned to where Chris was pointing and caught her breath when she recognised the man who had led the gang through the tunnels when they had been kidnapped. As the driver closed his van doors, he glanced casually over to where Chris and Mirela sat. The look of shock on his face when he saw the children was evidence enough that he also recognized them too. He darted to his vehicle, threw himself into the driving seat and took off in a cloud of dust.

Chris, dashed after the van, hoping to challenge him when he stopped to join the traffic at the main highway, but the van didn't stop. It careered out into the traffic without stopping, almost causing an accident. Chris tripped back to where Mirela was, furious that he had been unable to stop the man escaping.

When Joseph arrived shortly afterwards, the two children were able to tell him the news that Felix Gordeaux was still on the island and that they had his vehicle licence number.

"Good work," said Joseph. "He won't get far, Robert Dumas will have him in custody in no time. I'll wait in the car park and allow you to say your goodbyes."

He started to trudge away, then turning back, said, "By the way, did you ever find out which was the only rope on a sailing ship?" he asked quizzically, raising his eyebrows.

Chris and Mirela exchanged smiles, then said together, "Yes, it's the bell rope."

Joseph chuckled, "Of course it is. I'll see you in the car park Mirela. Good luck, Chris. I'm sure we will meet again."

Chris, looking down, scuffed his foot in the dust and looked sideways at Mirela, his reluctance plain to see as he realized that the moment to say their goodbyes had come. Bracing himself, he turned to Mirela and taking both her hands in his he looked solemnly into her eyes and said in a hoarse voice, "You take care of yourself Mirela, and I will see you again."

They hugged each other tightly, then releasing each other, Mirela smiled sadly and whispered, "Goodbye Chris."

He turned away, not wanting her to see how stricken he was, and stumbled toward his parent's car. A brief wave and then he was gone.

Rosanna appeared at Mirela's side and walked her towards where Joseph waited. "Don't be too sad my child," she said encouragingly. "I think you and Chris are destined to meet again often, and you will shape future events in many extraordinary ways."

The Three Fishers

Charles Kingsley (1819-75)
Three fishers went sailing out into the West,
Out into the West as the sun went down;
Each thought on the woman who loved him the best;
And the children stood watching them out of the town;
For men must work, and women must weep,
And there's little to earn and many to keep,
Though the harbour bar be moaning,
Three wives sat up in the light-house tower,
And trimmed the lamps as the sun went down;
They looked at the squall, and they looked at the shower,
And the night rack came rolling up ragged and brown,
But men must work, and women must weep,
Though storms be sudden, and waters deep,
And the harbour bar be moaning.
Three corpses lay out on the shining sands
In the morning gleam as the tide went down,
And women are weeping and wringing their hands
For those who will never come back to the town;
For men must work, and women must weep
And the sooner it's over, the sooner to sleep
and good-by to the bar and its moaning.

Book 'A GYPSY QUEST' approx. 50,000 words.

A supernatural adventure

Genre: Teenagers aged 11 to 15 years

Time period: Mid 1940s

PREVIOUSLY PUBLISHED WORK WITH POETRY NOW:

Silence in the Air. The Eternal Poppy 2003

The Cry of War. Armistice 2003

Poetry Now. Janet 2005

Monkey Business. Bess 2006

Mazes of the Mind. The Reprieve 2006

A Tapestry of Thoughts. The Safeguard 2010

Poetry Rivals. Mandela 2011

This Pleasant Land. Revival 2014

AUTHOR

William Carr

Email: Gwarffynonfarm@gmail.com

There is a copy of the poem 'The Three Fishers', the poem that Mirela dreams of while staying at the cottage where Charles Kingsley had previously lived, at the end of the manuscript.